C000301394

Gaia Servadio was born in Padua, Italy, in 1938. She moved to London in the 1950s to study graphic art, and has lived here ever since. Her first book, *Melinda*, was translated into nine languages and was an international bestseller. Her subsequent novels include *Don Juan*, *Il Metodo* and *La Vallata*, and she has also written three books on the Mafia and a book of memoirs on her Jewish childhood. She has written plays for Italian radio and is the author of several TV documentaries.

GAIA SERVADIO

the story of

TRANSLATED BY

ALLEGRA MOSTYN-OWEN

PAN BOOKS

LONDON, SYDNEY AND AUCKLAND

First British publication 1994 by Pan Books

a division of Pan Macmillan Publishers Limited
Cavaye Place London SW10 9PG
and Basingstoke

Associated companies throughout the world

ISBN 0 330 33203 1

Copyright © Gaia Servadio 1990

The right of Gaia Servadio to be identified as the
author of this work has been asserted by her in accordance
with the Copyright, Designs and Patents Act 1988.

All rights reserved. No reproduction, copy or transmission
of this publication may be made without written permission.
No paragraph of this publication may be reproduced, copied or
transmitted save with written permission or in accordance with
the provisions of the Copyright Act 1956 (as amended). Any
person who does any unauthorised act in relation to
this publication may be liable to criminal prosecution
and civil claims for damages.

1 3 5 7 9 8 6 4 2

A CIP catalogue record for this book is available from
the British Library

Phototypeset by Intype, London
Printed by Cox & Wyman Ltd, Reading, Berkshire

This book is sold subject to the condition that it shall not,
by way of trade or otherwise, be lent, re-sold, hired out,
or otherwise circulated without the publisher's prior consent
in any form of binding or cover other than that in which
it is published and without a similar condition including this
condition being imposed on the subsequent purchaser.

'Ce que son amant voulait d'elle était simple: qu'elle fût constamment et immédiatement accessible.'

Histoire d'O
by Pauline Réage

PART ONE

I

Spring was drawing to a close.

They were visiting their distant cousins the Beckfords for the first time. Actually, they were only cousins in a manner of speaking. Come to that, the Beckfords' home was only a house in a manner of speaking too: it was more like a mansion, a palace even. The two families lived only a few miles apart and Lockhart ladies had often been taken in marriage by Beckfords; it was how they came to be cousins – a rather distant connection but, in the country, everybody called each other cousin as long as they belonged to the same class – or nearly did.

The Beckfords lived in the most well-known castle in the neighbourhood. It was an old towering edifice, a medieval fortress which had been restored in the seventeenth century by one of the many bastard sons of the Royal House of Stuart.

Cranlie Hall was the ancestral home of the Lockharts, a family whose fortunes had been made in more recent times. It had been refurbished in the eighteen-hundreds with the addition of Regency porticos and impulsive Victorian turrets. But whereas the Lockharts hardly ever stayed at Cranlie Hall, the Beckfords were firmly rooted in Monpleasance even though circumstance and their own inertia had conspired to force them into selling off most of their holdings.

Polissena Lockhart had prepared herself carefully for the visit. She was familiar with the castle: she had come to see it a few years back when, as a newly-wed, she first visited the county. And she was already acquainted with the Beckfords, an elderly couple who fitted exactly her conception of the English as a species in decline.

The old marquis was an extremely handsome man. Shy and lean, clad in the rarest and most uncomfortable tweeds, he was almost afraid of the words he was able to string together with the help of a couple of dry martinis. Everything alien – and that included Polissena Braganza Lockhart – rather alarmed him. He had the habit of confusing those countries of Europe where different languages were spoken, where he had spent endless hours wandering around museums, churches and ruins, all of which he had instantly forgotten. He had sent his three sons to Eton and then on to Sandhurst in accordance with time-honoured tradition. In any case, they would never have managed to get through university; nor would the Beckfords ever have lowered themselves to that. Oxford and Cambridge were places for poofy intellectuals, so said the marquis, letting it be understood that 'intellectual' was in his view a far more damning epithet than 'poofy'.

The three daughters had gone to boarding schools in the country where they were taught the basics in how to land husbands. But Rowena, the second daughter, had never received a single marriage proposal in spite of the many bachelors whom the Beckfords had reluctantly invited to Monpleasance. Putting up with all those strangers at weekends had been such a strain that the marquis had ended up treating them extremely badly, demanding that they leave after tea on Saturday. On one occasion, he had even accused a young man of taking advantage of a snowstorm in order to stay for dinner.

Rowena tacitly blamed him but, as he surveyed her hairy upper lip, the old marquis reckoned that she had never enjoyed any serious matrimonial prospects.

The marquis' name was Roger Raymond (traditionally, all the Beckfords were christened with names beginning with the letter R). He was always mixing up Polissena's origins: he was not quite sure whether his cousin was Belgian or South African, or quite how many children she had produced with Cousin Oliver. There was also the matter of Polissena Lockhart having a job. In his day, women of his class never worked. At the most, they might breed horses, as his own wife had done on the understanding that she could squander most of the family inheritance in the process. Once upon a time, making money was frowned upon, and the old marquis had not yet realized that Mrs Thatcher's Britain had turned the tables on all of that. In any case, the Beckfords' considerable wealth had slipped irredeemably through the fingers of the latest generations: the land surrounding Monpleasance, an estate which had once seemed boundless, was sold off bit by bit to pay for

3

new horses, thieving butlers and incompetent cooks; and the Tudor farms were knocked down to make way for bargain bungalows.

The Beckfords had very nearly reached the end of the road: they were afflicted by that germ of decadence which somehow worms its way into the genes and the resolutions of every aristocratic family worth its salt. Having been educated to refrain from indulging in communication, the marquises of Beckford entertained very little; for several generations, they had been waiting for the only visit which really interested them, that is to say the monarch's. Had the great event ever actually come about, it would of course have stunned them: the Beckfords had forgotten the niceties of royal protocol long ago. They had not inherited a knack for extricating themselves from awkward situations; they neither knew how to interpret a menu, nor indeed how to issue orders, nor what to eat if they did. They had ended up leading a most comfortable existence.

In point of fact, the marchioness had already been boiling the salmon for several hours in preparation for the midday meal which was to be served in the dining room in the company of their six children and their cousins. As for trained cooks and impeccable domestic staff, these had disappeared from Monpleasance long before. A couple who occupied a wing of the castle succeeded in tyrannizing the marchioness Isabella to such an extent that they even refused to take the doggies for their ritual daily tour of the grounds. And certainly cooking was not one of the marchioness' more obvious accomplishments. Even the

4

vegetables – once they were unpacked from their plastic containers – had been tossed into boiling water several hours beforehand and were ready to be served up in a colourless and certainly tasteless condition.

II

Polissena paid great attention to what she would wear. A lunch in the country, in an austere house with people who seldom entertained. She chose a white silk blouse which she left unbuttoned at the throat and fastened with a brooch of pink topaz; a woollen skirt in a black and white check, some sensible shoes – no heel – and woollen stockings. She justly suspected that the room temperature at Monpleasance would be somewhat inferior to the temperature outside.

She completed the effect with a felt hat and a velvet jacket; she knew that she was irremediably different from them, the Beckfords, just as much as from the Lockharts. Polissena's was not a sensual face, but the body which stretched from the trim thighs and the slender hips to the high, firm though not over-large breasts betrayed the voluptuousness which was not in her eyes. She was a woman who could appear distant, sometimes dark and scowling. Professionally efficient, prone to being alternately overtaken by wild enthusiasm and uncontrollable impatience, she was easily bored; she would then withdraw into herself and assume a Japanese smile and a glazed stare. She combed herself in the mirror and decided upon how much make-up to apply for the occasion. She sprayed herself with a sweet-smelling oriental scent. 'Oliver?' she called her husband.

She was ready.

She would have to call Paris: it was Saturday. They were still working over there, not like in the English countryside.

The chauffeur was waiting for them. 'Do you remember our cousins the Beckfords?' Oliver asked her absent-mindedly as he seated himself democratically alongside the driver, leaving her alone on the back seat to ease herself into the blue cushions. There, she let herself sway with the suspension: it gave her a gentle tingling pleasure between her legs.

Not that Oliver really was democratic. He was counting on the impact which his arrival would create on his nobler and poorer cousins. Louis was not actually his employee, but there was no need to mention that.

'. . . a couple of years ago, but I don't think Cousin Isabella was there.' The gravel crunched under the wheels of the Mercedes. He was wrong, Polissena reflected; she and Isabella had already met at one of those drinks parties where you were offered soggy canapés and everyone stood around not talking about anything much. Pale and thin, with a Myrna Loy hair-do, an incomprehensible accent and a perm on top of her blue rinse, the marchioness Isabella's beauty had not yet worn off.

Polissena thought about her afternoon schedule. She would return to London in order to leave again for Frankfurt. Louis would be sent on to Paris alone and she would take the plane. She was amused by the idea of lunch at Monpleasance. 'Do they have any children?'

'Six, all grown-up of course. The eldest, Lord Rupert, is rather ugly – he must be your age. Then there's Rudolph, and the third . . . I can't remember his name. He too must be called something beginning with R., like the rest of them. Then there's the three girls, one ugly one, and the other two indifferent; they wanted to hitch me up with one of them . . .'

Polissena looked out at the English countryside sliding along the road. It was an affected kind of landscape: the estates of the gentry mimicked a wilder country; the hills were unable to lift themselves up and seemed to buckle beneath the weight of the barley, the oats and the beech hedges.

'How much is a Caravaggio worth?' asked Oliver out of the blue. It was the kind of question which invariably irritated Polissena. Her heart-shaped, highly painted, pouting lips stiffened with annoyance.

'There aren't any on the market,' she replied, 'so there's no point wasting time thinking about it.'

Oliver looked out of the window. She had begun to find him disagreeable. He was one of those sham workers from the City who – sooner or later – would be swept aside by the Thatcher revolution, the type who thought big but was not prepared to make the effort. He was a terrible snob.

'You're wrong: there are some,' he said. 'I've teamed up with some friends and we're thinking of buying them.

We'll set up a company, sell off one of them and store the rest in a bank for the next twenty years, or maybe sell one at auction . . .'

'The rest of them? I can't believe there are that many Caravaggios in circulation . . . The moment one turns up, you know it must be stolen: Caravaggio's the kind of painter who's never been out of fashion. His canvases are all catalogued; we know everything there is to know about him. I can't see what the deal is unless it's something crooked.'

Oliver turned a stony face towards her. 'If we do clinch this deal, it has to remain a secret.'

There was no danger on that score as his wife promptly forgot what he told her anyway. Indeed she was now looking out at the countryside: her velvety eyes were mobile and her ears looked bored. Everything Oliver said was irritating: his snobbery, his arrogance. Fortunately they did not spend much time together. Although he exploited her position, Oliver would not admit to himself or to others that he was too lazy to get what he most wanted: fame and success.

Monpleasance stood out on a slope against a series of hillocks surrounded by a lake which could only just be glimpsed. The drive into the park was barred by a hostile lodgekeeper. 'Mr Lockhart?' They were expected.

As with all those grandiose estates, the drive traced a fatuous route, as extensive as possible so as to intimidate new arrivals with the vastness of the holdings. Great oaks and chestnuts grew densely in the woods about which pheasants and rabbits scuttled in their thousands.

Oliver was holding forth.

God only knew what he was saying. Was he addressing her or the driver? He was relating gossip to her, things he had picked up in the newspaper and pretended were first-hand news, or stories which she herself had told him, a source he would invariably forget . . .

'Our dear cousin!' the marchioness, who hardly knew her, welcomed her. She was wearing an amazonian outfit and was followed by a small horde of dogs. The Marchioness of Beckford feigned not to look at her cousin as she studied her greedily: there was not much to do in the country. Polissena, who was much younger than the marchioness, was a favourite topic of telephonic gossip: the marchioness regularly discussed how she carried off her success with charm and Oliver with detachment. Cousin Oliver did not seem much changed: tall and egocentic, he only talked about himself or about those who knew him; in other words, he was a useless appendage. She had always hoped to marry him off to one of her daughters, first to Reena, then Rowena, then Roberta: the Lockharts were wealthy, even if the family stock was not altogether desirable.

The Marquis of Beckford embraced both the new arrivals with practised detachment. He offered them a martini dry; Polissena watched its voluptuous preparation in a 1930s cocktail shaker from which it was then poured into glass beakers.

Standing next to the fireplace were two men; another was seated on the paisley-covered sofa. 'Rupert,' announced his father, as he introduced her to the eldest; 'our cousin has come to visit us with Cousin Oliver.'

He had clearly forgotten her name. Polissena came to

his rescue and extended her arm to grasp the rather limp hand of Lord Rupert. In that house, everyone always forgot everyone else's name . . .

'And Rudolph . . . his wife is out hunting in aid of charity today. Rudolph, meet our cousin,' said the marquis. Polissena was unable to catch the name of the third. All she saw was a straight nose, a small, slightly shark-like mouth and two blue eyes which flashed at her rapidly, agitatedly.

'It's the cousins' wedding tomorrow,' the marchioness announced. 'I suppose everyone will be there.' All the country folk, especially those who intermarried, thought Polissena. Oliver would be going.

'Polissena's going back to London this very evening,' countered Oliver, 'for her work.'

'Oh! You poor thing! And in that ghastly traffic too!' wailed the Marchioness Isabella.

'Having a chauffeur allows me to rest.'

'Have you got any room to spare? Are you going alone? You could give a lift to . . .' and the old marquis gestured in the direction of his third son who timorously raised his blue, intensely blue eyes at her. He kept them hidden under his eyelids almost as though they were a treasure that he wanted to conceal. Again he lifted his long lashes from his wet irises: the clear gaze of those eyes addressed her timidly. He did not utter a word – just as if he had frozen up.

Polissena wondered whether cousin R. was always that shy or whether it was her presence which had this effect on him given that the look of his intense blue eyes attracted her with such unexpected force. She tried not to look hard at him, not even to glance at him because as soon as she met his gaze, his blue eyes would burrow beneath those large lids like a frightened gazelle.

At table, as they picked at the predictable fare – it was sliced grapefruit – Polissena pretended to listen to the conversation which may or may not have been general; instead she thought of that timid look which brought to mind the wilful demands of her own body. A strong electric charge seemed to attack her from the other side of the table, unleashed in those looks which coincided every now and then. They did not talk to one another.

'Would you like to have a look around the house?' the marquis enquired of Polissena, as with particular courtesy, he spilt the coffee on to the saucer and the tray, leaving very little for the cup itself. 'The rooms with the William Kent furniture have been restored. Rupert, why don't you take Cousin Oliver to see the Adam rooms,' and, emboldened by the martini drys, he took Polissena by the arm. 'You, dear cousin, will come with me to gaol! But mind you don't shut the gate down there as I'm the only one with the key!'

They went out in a group to have a look at the old castle prison. There might have been some beautiful paintings left in the castle's picture galleries: there should have been in this kind of family, but they were probably unaware of owning any. She had heard of a Georges de la Tour mentioned at one time but maybe they had sold it by now.

11

The steps had been carved out of the bedrock and led down to two deep and dark labyrinths. Ungainly Rowena, together with Reena and R., was holding up a torch to show the others the way down, and to highlight the instruments of torture with the familiarity and half-heartedness which comes of repeating the same things many times over. The chains, which hung from rings wedged into the walls, were the subject of pleasurably cruel description, to which the marquis would add a new insight made up on the spur of the moment, no doubt in order to fend off his boredom. R. listened and, in the gloom, his eyes darkened to an almost Prussian blue.

They descended the last steps. The stones glistened with moisture: rats had certainly plagued those ancient and hopeless prisoners whom the marquises of Beckford had sent to their deaths. These days, all those Rs would not have hurt a fly, but it was clear that that was the result of inactivity rather than goodness on their part.

They climbed up again after the relation of a few more vicious, inhuman and savage details. You could barely see your way up the spiral staircase.

Polissena was last behind R. who lit up her path, pointing the torch at the steps. She took in R.'s glossy brown hair, grown slightly long around the base of the neck and curly around his small ears, like a classical sculpture. She could feel the attraction of his presence; she wanted to touch him and to be touched.

The others had now reached the surface. You could hear their voices disperse above in distant garrulous murmurs, and then finally disappear.

'Let's go back,' ordered Polissena.

R. jerked around at the sound of her voice.

'I dropped something,' she added.

This time the light was behind her shoulders and R. could observe her closely; he saw the silhouette of her round breasts heave a little as she went down the spiral staircase. Almost not daring to, he looked at her legs descending the tight bends of the steps. Once they had arrived at the bottom, Polissena bent down to search and R. lit up the ground with the torch.

She felt the wet stone. In the silence, their breath smoked against the torchlight and misted up the dark air. R. felt Polissena's hand on his knee – was it a mistake? But no, her hand stayed there, hot through the fabric covering his legs; the other hand had left off searching and was moving up the other leg, touching his strong calves and then moving on slowly, along his knees and on his thighs as he stiffened; he felt as if he were made of stone.

Polissena could feel an ecstatic frenzy propelling the hands which sought the middle of those legs: the torch had fallen to the ground.

She raised herself to her feet and her mouth sought R.'s as her hand unbuckled his belt and unbuttoned his trousers. She could feel the rigid heat swollen with desire beneath her touch. She grazed the hot tender tip and then, with both her hands, she looked for the hard pulsating base of his sex. She kneeled down and gripped his legs between her arms and looked for him with her mouth, licking him lightly, then swallowing and sucking him. His trousers had slipped to the ground and now Polissena slowly peeled off

13

his underpants from his body. R. was naked from the waist down: his body was offered up to her mouth. The tip of her bosom stiffened against him as if she were trying to penetrate R.'s legs in the same way that he was now penetrating her mouth.

R.'s involuntary groans excited her; as her excitement nailed down the base of her belly, she was inundated by a warm liquid which bathed her skirt. She was surprised: she had never before come so abundantly. The more R. swelled inside her mouth, the more her belly, her thighs, her hands became inflamed.

She sensed that R. could hardly stay on his feet any longer: he was swaying. Polissena's hands ran up his arching back and up his broad, smooth chest. Filled with desire, she kissed him in the mouth. He was trembling; his hard erect member cleaved the air between those solid great legs stretched wide apart and silhouetted in the torchlight. She touched the curves of his buttocks and pressed her hand into the soft recesses of his thighs, entering his hot and secret folds with her fingers, and pushing against R.'s tension with her clothed body.

Then she rose and slammed shut the cell door behind her. The bolt clicked home automatically, leaving R. on the other side.

'Mrs Lockhart!' R. called out in the darkness: there was a quiver of fear in his voice.

'Come here.'

It was their first verbal exchange.

Kneeling once again, Polissena thrust her face between

the bars; again she took his hot swollen member in her mouth and sucked him, causing him to totter as he leant against the bars to stop himself from falling. Her mouth began to move across his stomach, only to return to sucking him until R. could no longer restrain his pleasure, and his orgasm burst into her mouth. Almost at once, Polissena's voice came back to him. 'For this you must be punished.'

But why? thought R.: what had he done wrong? He saw that she was picking up the torch from the ground. 'Are you taking it away? You're leaving me alone?' Polissena looked at his blue eyes staring at her in the penumbra.

'I'll have to get your father to give me the key if what he said is true. You'll have to stay in prison in the meantime.'

His virile, vibrant voice excited her. The stream of light shone on his bare loins and his flat knees. Through the bars, Polissena stroked the hairs curled over his spent member.

She was going to have another coffee with the marquis and Lady Isabella, with those fat sons, horsy daughters and the dogs before extracting the key from his parent and returning to Monpleasance prison.

She was going to make him suffer.

That was the way she liked it.

III

She had sent Louis to fetch him.

Her baggage was already in the boot of the Mercedes and the telephone lay at the ready on the fake mahogany sidetable. But with R. beside her, how was she going to get any work done? For a moment, she felt a sense of dread: after what had passed between them earlier on that afternoon, would he have found some excuse not to travel with her? Would he fear her proximity?

She was reassured by the sight of the blue Mercedes returning loaded with its precious cargo. R. had the appearance of one who has been found guilty: he kept his eyes lowered and would not look at her.

Polissena asked whether he wanted some tea, a glass of champagne or an espresso coffee before they embarked on their journey. It would take a couple of hours: they would get to London at about half past nine in the evening. 'No thanks,' murmured R., with his eyes lowered as before.

'Then let's go at once,' she ordered dryly, addressing Louis at well as R.

R.'s paralytic shyness gave her a sense of power. She wanted to overcome him, to draw him into the game and to dominate him. Nestling in the soft blue interior of the car, R. let himself imagine the body of the woman sitting beside him. He recalled the intense and unexpected pleasure of that afternoon; nothing like it had ever happened to him before. The gentle, luxurious motion of the car, the dark country outside, her scent — all this gave him a sense of new adventure. But he feared her; he never knew what to expect from her.

Polissena lifted up the telephone receiver and he smiled at her as if to say that he had enjoyed the events of that afternoon, including her trick of leaving him locked up inside a damp prison cell. He looked at her blouse, left open down to the crease of her breast and he glimpsed the full, round bosom. He felt his legs tickle with desire and pleasure at the sweet thought of those warm curves which he had not yet explored.

'Dauphine?' she called into the telephone. 'I'm coming back tonight. I'll be home in a couple of hours. Tell the doorman to expect me. And book a ticket for me on the flight to Frankfurt tomorrow afternoon; I may not actually need to go — it all depends on the outcome of the morning's meetings. Better still, why don't you book two more tickets, and see whether you and Valentina can't come too? Don't forget to confirm tomorrow's meetings early on, will you? . . . Come off it! Do you really think that anyone at Sotheby's or Christie's will be at their desks before nine?' She smiled and the telephone returned to silence.

'That was my secretary,' she explained, stroking his hand. She scrutinized R.'s profile, with its delicate nose over those thin lips. Even side on, she still had a good view of the luminous blue of his eyes filtering through his long lashes; she took in the gentleness of his small hands, resting shyly on his legs, and his embarrassed attitude towards her. It filled Polissena with desire, with the will to conquer and

17

subdue that man whose name she had not yet grasped. She touched him between his legs and felt that he was already ready. She unbuttoned his trousers and held him with both her hands. R. shook his head and motioned towards Louis, but Polissena did not seem in the least bit bothered by R.'s silent signals. She massaged his testicles with an expert lightness of touch as she kissed him on the mouth with renewed violence. Polissena could feel the waves of her own desire beating against her lower belly. She had known that pants were only going to be a nuisance during the car journey and, in fact, she was not wearing any. The tip of her breast again grew hard against R.'s chest. Frantically, she undid his shirt and slid her hands along his back. Polissena's mouth was glued against R.'s; his worried, gazing eyes could not avoid looking at the chauffeur's shoulders only a few inches away from their panting heap.

Louis could not not hear, not follow, not understand every sigh and gasp and movement. R. wondered whether Louis was used to this kind of bustle in the back of the car, whether Polissena always did this kind of thing with her travelling companions, whether her journeys were nothing but erotic dances and transient couplings in the back of the blue Mercedes.

On the one hand, he was troubled by the thought that had just struck him: the idea that Polissena gave herself to others and did so often, provoked his jealousy. But as he thought of this, he realized that he had not yet actually possessed her, that she was the one who had taken him from that calculated distance between the locked bars of the ancestral prison.

She had seated herself on R.'s knees. He could feel her legs opening on to her wet centre of longing as his burning desire found her. They rocked in unison, finding a common rhythm straight away, as if already used to one another. R. lengthened and thickened within her, and Polissena melted into him and then pushed against him as though she wanted to possess him, rather than to be possessed. She ate him with her mouth: with her tongue, she entered into his ears; her lips lingered on his cheekbones and his eyelids, and then returned to penetrate his small and delicate mouth.

R.'s hands were on her bosom. Her breasts stiffened beneath his touch as his fingers rotated about her round, swollen curves; she was still melting on top of him. R. was worried: would he be able to climax sufficiently discreetly and silently so as not to make things too obvious? But Polissena was not at all disturbed by Louis' presence. What was this woman doing to him? They were about to drive through London, piled up on one another, inside each other. He was almost afraid at the thought that Polissena was going to make him do this and more: she was capable of anything. With an effort, he pushed himself into her. Unable to contain himself any longer, he emptied himself into her belly as Louis continued coasting down the motorway.

IV

She had made him remove his trousers. He was wearing socks, shoes, shirt and jacket. They were crossing Battersea Bridge. 'I love you,' she told him. His blue eyes looked at her in astonishment.

King's Road was drenched with rain. The shop windows were crowded with extravagant dummies and unwearable clothes; their lights illuminated his straddled legs; the street lamps of Sloane Square picked out the shadows of R.'s face from above. 'If you love me, you have to obey me.' She stroked his naked sex and he responded to her touch. 'You'll come and stay with me tonight. Tomorrow we're going to Frankfurt.' She wanted to kidnap him.

'I can't: I have to go and see a friend. I came purposely to clinch a deal: he's coming to do some shooting at Monpleasance . . .' He did not even know where they were heading.

The Mercedes cruised towards Hyde Park and turned into Piccadilly. 'Do you love me?'

R. looked at her again in astonishment. They had met that very day. But he knew he wanted to live out the physical and emotional adventure which Polissena offered him. He sensed that he was not allowed to ask questions, that – on the contrary – any questions on his part would have been out of place. Louis did not bother him any more. The blue-uniformed chauffeur had been driving for two hours without reacting minimally to the movements of his passengers. Yet he was young and red-blooded – if you could ever describe a Belgian as such. Maybe he had been overwhelmed by their desire but had nonetheless managed to maintain a certain absent-minded distance; maybe such detachment was something to which he was accustomed.

Polissena – whom Louis referred to as Madame Braganza – allowed R. to get dressed again before the Mercedes drove into Albany Yard: she kept a small flat on the first floor, staircase B. She told the driver to go and rest, but to be sure to find himself in front of the Albany on the following day at three o'clock in the afternoon. 'I'll manage without you in the morning,' she told him. She used familiar tones with her chauffeur, and he answered with reserve. She clasped her cape with one hand and, with the other, she took R.'s arm and made her triumphal entrance into the Albany's internal corridor leading to staircase B.

V

'You must be hungry,' she said to him, after laying down her papers on the bed. She looked at him with admiration. She liked his squarish body, the imperial Roman head, the brown curls, the surprise in those blue eyes of his.

He nodded.

'Let's go down to Green's. We'll have some oysters out of season. Let's celebrate.' She was authoritarian and rather moody.

'What are we celebrating?' asked R. with ignorant temerity.

'Us, of course: having found each other.'

R. wanted to ask her how many men she had 'found' and played with in the same way, but he did not dare. He knew hardly anything about Polissena apart from their distant kinship and that she had a house near Monpleasance where he had gone shooting once or twice. He was aware that she was married to Oliver, a man he scarcely knew, partly because Oliver was at least twenty years his senior: he also knew that Polissena must be quite a few years older than him. You could tell by her ways, rather than by her looks.

He looked her in the face and smiled; as he did so, R.'s molars showed Dracula-like between his lips. It was something which Polissena had already taken in with languorous delight.

That fine and quiet mouth of his was an object of penetration. She had looked for it with her tongue and her fingers; she pledged herself again to look inside his mouth and do it violence.

Without even kissing each other, they went out under the rain, crossed Piccadilly and skirted the windows of Fortnum & Mason, which looked like chocolate boxes bursting with knick-knacks and bows: then they turned down Duke Street and came to Green's.

The restaurant was still packed with couples and afflu-ent little groups. The drawings hanging on the walls were meant to set off the sense of well-being and upper-middle-class good taste which pervaded the restaurant. Even the colours – rich reds and dark greens – stimulated a Pavlovian recognition of the nineteenth-century English club setting. She had not taken him there to impress him, but because she liked to eat oysters, and Green's was around the corner from home. In any case, all the restaurants in that area were horribly expensive.

A waiter approached them. 'Madame Braganza!' he welcomed her in a discreet and harmonious, rather exotic drawl which sounded Polish. No one knew her as Lockhart, reflected R. They called her by a name which rang new, mysterious and alien. How was it that they knew her? And how would he manage the bill? R. only had about thirty pounds in his pocket and, though the credit cards which he possessed were several and brightly coloured too, this merely glossed over his straitened circumstances; he certainly could not allow himself to go to this kind of restaurant. R. had always wanted to have money, but he had not yet succeeded in making any. As the youngest, he was not entitled to anything under English law.

The waiter led the way. 'Your usual table, Madame. Shall I bring the menu?'

'No. Just give us the usual, and a bottle of champagne – not a vintage.'

She was doing everything. R. looked at her quizzically but without hostility. 'I've ordered oysters,' she reassured him.

Polissena had a heart-shaped mouth over which she had applied a layer of creamy, fuchsia-coloured lipstick. She wore a white silk scarf around her neck which was fastened by a beautiful and doubtless genuine jewel. Not that R. noticed; he did not notice many things. He was not used to it: no one had ever taught him to observe things, and he was still too young to have acquired that kind of culture by himself. Perhaps he was the type who would never learn to observe. Or to think.

Polissena's hands were larger than R.'s and her shoulders also had something masculine about them, though they did enclose that firm, round bosom. Just looking at her breasts filled him with a longing to squeeze and touch them. She smiled at him: after half a bottle of champagne, he was going to be less timorous.

She had changed her shoes. She was now wearing a pair of high heels in black patent leather; they tapered her calf and made her look taller than him. The change of shoes had made her more feminine: it had given her an almost vulgar way of walking which contrasted markedly with the severity of her expression. 'It's almost too late to raise the subject,' she informed him, 'but I'll tell you straight away that I haven't got AIDS.'

He thought he had not heard her properly: this was not the sort of thing you talked about in restaurants. 'And what about you?'

She took his hand under the table between the rich folds of the tablecloth and massaged his fingertips and his cuticles. R.'s hand suddenly stiffened. 'There's someone I know here,' he told her.

'So what?'

'I'm not used to being seen in public . . . touching a lady.'

Polissena burst out laughing. Once ladies used to be the ones who had to keep their tender exchanges hidden from prying eyes.

A young man stationed himself before them. He had an air about him and a way of speaking of someone repressed, conventional and derisory. 'Well, well! If it isn't Reading Minor. Where've you been hiding yourself away then, you old rascal? Always at Monpleasance, eh?' He was one of those types who always spoke in exclamations, the kind who likes to hear the sound of his own laughter. 'We must meet up. How about a spot of shooting in Scotland?' Out of shyness and Anglo-Saxon habit, the stranger had not yet even glanced at Polissena.

'I haven't got my guns with me – I left them at home.'

'Larking about then, are we, eh?' He had not introduced her. Maybe he was embarrassed by her. Or maybe he was ashamed of her seeing him with this character who filled his mouth with breathy aitches – so typically the county squire. Most likely he was embarrassed by her, she who spoke with very few breathy aitches and who never dreamt of going shooting.

The oysters arrived. The intruder gave her a sidelong glance. He had been brought up and educated not to look at women; he belonged to that tribe of Etonians who had learnt to exclude everything they did not understand. At last he left them, conceding her a couple of incomprehensible syllables which could be construed as a leave-taking.

25

A plate of twelve pearly, honey-coloured oysters lay before them. They had been delicately cut out of the shells upon which they rested and now they stared at Polissena and R. with the glazed look of a martyred saint. Alone once more, they smiled at each other.

'Madame Braganza?' Nicholas Newman held out his hand towards her.

Polissena replaced the loaded shell which she had anticipated swallowing with delight.

'It is such a pleasure to see you, Newman. We're meeting tomorrow: I trust you've received confirmation via my secretary.'

How was she going to introduce R.? She could not remember his name: come to that, she had never grasped it in the first place. But she knew the surname: Reading.

'Meet Nicholas Newman, director of the National Gallery.'

R. mumbled his own name.

'Reading?' queried Newman, who knew everything and had a very sharp sense of hearing. 'Reading? The Beckford family? Of Monpleasance?'

'Yes,' replied R. who was stunned by such breadth of knowledge.

'Do you still own that magnificent Lorenzo Lotto?' R. did not have the faintest idea about what had stayed in place at Monpleasance and what had been sold off. No one ever looked at anything in his family. No one had ever told him what there was in that vast mansion which had been plundered through years of debt and ignorance. It has to be said that he had never shown any curiosity either. He knew that many canvases had been flogged to dubious dealers who had introduced themselves to the marchioness, his grandmother, with whole suitcases stuffed with bank notes.

'I wouldn't know,' he responded disarmingly.

'And what about the Poussins? There were two in the study I seem to recall, as well as a splendid Bellotto . . .' The Poussins certainly were not there any more: Polissena would have recognized them. Poussin was her special subject.

'Maybe they went in the Sotheby's sale back in '72.' R. was taken aback by Newman's knowledge. Newman was taken aback by R.'s ignorance. Had he not been just an object, Polissena would have been embarrassed at being found in such company by the director of the most important museum in the country. But by this stage Newman had begun to suspect that the Louvre was after what little remained at Monpleasance.

'I'll have the Georges de la Tour,' he announced to her. Polissena made no answer: she had not even seen it. 'It's in England and it won't ever leave England, eh? Am I right?'

Polissena looked at him with a smile. There was no doubt about it: the de la Tour would come to the Louvre.

The quirky cut of Newman's suit and his ashen complexion intrigued R. 'Can I sit down?' asked Newman, seating himself on a comfortable armchair without further ado. 'There'll be two of us at the meeting tomorrow; they're idiots who know nothing but who have to be kept sweet.

27

They don't understand exhibitions; they'd like to put on easy, lightweight stuff, and then it's down to us to answer to the critics, eh? Am I right? The public isn't stupid either: they come to exhibitions only if they're interesting and if what we offer them is good quality. We can easily find a sponsor then, eh? I'm right, aren't I? I'm convinced of it.'

'But what are they suggesting instead?' asked Polissena.

'They're suggesting we should spend less and tell the story of London in pretty little pictures. As if we didn't have interesting works to put on show, nor much to say! My view is either we put on a Hogarth show or we organize an exhibition about the British School, no? Am I right? Come on!' he had a whole string of expressions which seemed to absorb all his nervous energies. 'In effect, well, surely.'

'I'll have to consult our curators. Besides, we haven't really got anything for you. We'd happily put on a Hogarth exhibition at the Petit Palais but it would have to wait four years. If you take three years putting it together, finding sponsors, making up the catalogue – which we would have to translate and, if we didn't like it, we'd make up another *ex novo* – the exhibition would then come to us the following year. But I'll tell you straight off: the two pieces you may be counting on can't possibly leave the Louvre: that's one of the matters for tomorrow's talks . . .'

'You never give us anything we ask for and on top of that, French catalogues are always a total disaster, eh? Am I not right? So many meaningless words, hot air, nebulous terms, penned by academics who seem only to want to see their names in print, with names a mile long, contradicting themselves within a single sentence, eh? It's true, isn't it?' Seeking confirmation for the truths he was telling, Newman turned to R. 'It's true, isn't it? No? Aren't I right? Don't you agree?'

'I wouldn't know,' said R. who was stunned by their conversation, by the strange names, by the kind of problem at hand and, above all, that anyone should be asking for his opinion.

'As you know, French laws are pretty stiff. I can't complain but sometimes I have to accept certain limitations because, if the Louvre doesn't lend out, none of the other museums will be generous to us either. I'm always saying as much to the minister . . .' said Polissena.

'Then make sure you help me over the Hogarth: you're important; these people believe that you're some kind of—'

'What? And you? What do you believe?'

'Madame! I admire you enormously. Really, I mean it seriously, you know that, yes, absolutely! Without a doubt!' He got up, springing up nervously, just as he had done when he had first sat down, said goodbye swallowing his syllables and left with his jacket hanging from his back like some Andalusian mantle and his tie pressed flat on his chest like a pancake.

'He's very good,' Polissena commented; 'I trust his judgement. Besides, don't you think he's right? Hogarth is a great painter whom everyone wants to get to know better, but what do you do with the British School in its widest sense? A British School! Let's not talk rot. There's no such thing!'

R. was looking at her as though she were some form of Dadaist sculpture, as though she were using surreal arguments. In point of fact, he had no clue what she was talking about. Polissena would doubtless have reacted in the same way if R. had started discussing shotguns and rifles.

At last she bit into the oyster which had lain abandoned on her plate. With her knee, she pushed against R.'s leg as, with her pointed shoes, she drew R.'s foot towards her.

'Watch out or they'll see us!'

'Who then? What's it to you anyway?'

VI

At last they were alone in the pleasantly warm room. Their hair was damp from the drizzle. They were standing by the big bed which took up most of the room.

Polissena took his head between her hands and stroked his chestnut curls, touching his cheekbones and rubbing her thighs against him. At last they were no longer exposed to the eyes of others. The champagne tickled his temples and his swollen desire pressed against its cloth confinement. R. clutched her; looking for the curves of her legs and thighs, he pulled her shoulders towards his chest. Those heels lifted her so high that, by bending down only slightly,

R. could kiss the breasts he sought. He opened up her shirt and unfastened her bra.

Polissena removed his tie; he wore cufflinks. His chest was bare at last. It gave way to a short, thick neck; below, his crotch sprouted with curls which were lighter in colour than his hair. R.'s skin was otherwise smooth. Polissena kissed him passionately, transportedly. She had never liked the hairiness of some great Latin chests, or muscular arms or virile calves for that matter.

His trousers were falling down.

'Now take your shoes off,' she ordered him, 'and remove your socks. Take off your underpants, that's right.'

He was completely naked in front of her and she was fully dressed on top of those high heels. Young and strong as he was, he wanted to penetrate her straight away. There was in him a lack of experience, of erotic technique which she found seductive.

He lifted Polissena's skirt and, finding her naked, he shifted her suspenders and felt for the wetness he had just touched with his fingers as he prepared her for the attack. She rocked on her heels and pushed him from above, squeezing her body against his stomach whilst the bud of his sex grew inside her body like a tulip. R. leant against the foot of the bed to help himself take her from below, forgetting that he would have wanted to enjoy her slowly.

R. never came noisily; he sighed with his eyes closed and, as soon as he reached climax, his member withdrew as if scared off. That hot, throbbing, wine-coloured object of desire with its soft and velvety head like a turgid mushroom, had immediately afterward assumed the consistency of an octopus and the wet softness of a cuttlefish.

'You didn't wait for me,' she scolded him.

He looked doubly naked with his shrunken penis before Polissena, dressed up in her heels and taller than him.

'Stay where you are,' she ordered him. Without undressing, Polissena lay down on the bed. 'Now turn towards me. Look at me.' From the brass footboard of the Victorian bed, R. had an oblique and close-up view of her open legs and her sombre but ecstatic face. In the shadow of the skirt which Polissena had brushed aside with her hand, R. could guess at her more secret parts. With the index finger of her tense hand extended between her legs, Polissena gently pressed and caressed herself with increasing intensity as a mysterious smile played on her lips. She looked like a Santa Teresa sculpted by Bernini with those fixed, ecstatic eyes and her breath coming in short gasps. It was as if R. did not exist. She was gasping for air and, every now and then, she would stop to catch her breath as though she had run short of oxygen. Tensed in her own pleasure, she concentrated on that one hand, on the hot gushes which bathed her legs and the bedclothes every time she came. With her left hand she stroked her stiffening breasts. She was behaving like a man, thought R. He felt out of his depth; all he could do was watch her and feel as useless as if he had found himself faced by some unknown couple making love. He was excited by that pulsating body which offered itself to him, at the sight of those uncensored details, violent, almost obstetric details. Her pleasure and her relish in violating his eyes with her onanism excited him. Not that he articulated such thoughts, but he understood that, in some way, Polissena was raping him.

She derived intense pleasure from opening herself up to R.'s gaze, from showing herself offered up yet unobtainable before his erect manhood, stretched out towards her in useless expectation. The hand between her legs moved increasingly frantically and jerkily. Polissena parted her lips and thrust her belly towards the ceiling as if seeking a man to penetrate her from above. R. could feel his desire reawakening. The blood rushed to his groin, pressing at him and swelling him. Polissena's breath came ever more gasping; the tension broke in one long, liberating spasm like a man's, as Polissena's eyes remained half open and her teeth glistened like pearls. She had wet her skirt and her savage smell excited R. From behind the end of the bed, he reached into the centre of her pleasure and attempted to prolong the caress which had brought her to such a powerful climax. 'Wait,' she told him: 'no.'

He could not understand why she was so excited by the idea of masturbating before him, of violating his sense of modesty as she opened up her body and exposed those orgasmic and exultant convulsions which left her wet and open to the scrutiny of a man she hardly knew. 'No,' she repeated: 'no.'

Perhaps she was behaving in this way because R. was nothing more than an object before which she felt no shame; that was why his forcibly passive testimony redoubled the joy she derived from freeing her sexual tension

33

privately and on her own. He was passive because that was what she wanted. 'Wait,' she told him again.

She began to touch herself, to stroke herself with her other hand, pressing herself in a different spot; every point yielded a distinct sensation. Like a multi-faceted diamond picking out a ray of light according to its position, so the tip of Polissena's hand played with the subtlety and sophistication of an acutely sensitive organ. Her entire body coiled around her hand and, this time, Polissena exploded at once. R. helped her to undress and, as he removed her blouse, she went on touching herself, stroking herself, violently, then gently, and coming in spasms which aroused in R. a mixture of desire and rage. It was as if Polissena was declaring herself self-sufficient, as if she had no need of him. But he wanted her badly and showed it by the abundance of his own desire hardened before her.

Her blouse dropped to the ground, then her shiny silk bra. Her neck was delicately divided by a necklace of pearl and topaz which sparkled in the gloom like the saliva on her teeth, between her parted lips. She felt like an Olympia or a consenting Maya Desnuda. R. unrolled her stockings with his face over her juddering hand and only a few inches from her orgasm; at her every movement, his hard sex touched her body and pressed against it.

'Look at me.'

She had begun to caress herself again, first with her left hand, then with both together. Men could not know the secret of her pleasure. Now she was unable to hold back. As she came in increasingly shattering orgasms, she would begin once more in front of his blue gaze. R. licked her breasts as she came again for the sixth, for the seventh time and, as R. sought to take her, she repulsed him. At last, gasping, R. entered into her belly. The night was consumed between them: if he fell asleep after taking her from the side as she curled her legs up around his waist, or had R. on top of her with his knees pressed into the mattress, then she would wake him: it was her turn. She would suck him: she wanted to be taken again. She touched him, stroked him, and her mouth locked into his. 'From now on, you have to dress in such a way as always to be at my disposal,' Polissena suddenly told him. 'You won't wear cufflinks as they take too long to undo, nor will you wear buttons on your trousers – only zips.'

Zips were anathema to a man like R. who was much more careful about this kind of detail than about others which were far more important. He looked at her in surprise. 'You will obey me, won't you?'

They did not speak during the pauses, but looked at one another in the shadowy light. Under his admiring gaze, Polissena touched his ears and the softer parts of his body and she touched the strong calves of her pagan God. It did not matter at all that they had nothing to say to one another, that they shared no common language. For they had discovered a different one.

Sunlight was filtering through the curtains when R. woke up exhausted; from the thin, diaphanous light, he guessed that it was probably raining outside. The splashing of a shower came from the bathroom. He got up to take her in his arms. But he had got it wrong: it was the noise of rain pouring down a gutter and spraying one of the window panes.

Polissena had gone out to keep her business appointments.

VII

Louis came to collect him; his blue uniform was starched perfectly. Being rather taller than R., he bent down slightly as he opened the door in an effort not to overwhelm him with his height. R. felt somewhat embarrassed even though Louis expertly – too expertly – looked at him as if he had never seen, heard, or understood a thing.

Louis did notice that Mr Reading's smile had changed, though observation was not a feature of his job, or of his nationality; on the contrary, it was his business not to want to take in the reason for the change that had come over R. Mr Reading struck him as more self-confident, though not quite natural; but the English never did behave naturally under such circumstances. Louis knew nothing about the English, and all the clichés he had ever heard about them seemed to correspond exactly with what he had had occasion to notice himself.

'Bonjour!' exclaimed R. with such an exaggerated accent that, for an instant, Louis did not understand which language he was using.

'Good day, Mr Reading! Here's a bit of fine weather at last after all that rain.' He wanted to seem affable and to make chauffeur-like conversation. It was second nature to him anyway.

Where were they going? What did Polissena have in store for him? She had kidnapped him and he had played the part of a frightened Proserpina to her threatening Pluto. He did not know what to think of her, though he could do nothing but think about her: her perfumed skin, her back and sensuous eyes, her round curves and exotic accent.

'We'll be going with her personal secretary to pick up her other secretary and then we're driving directly to the airport. Madame Braganza said she hoped you would excuse her: she would have preferred to be with you.'

R. should not have asked questions of one of Polissena's employees but he wanted information. 'Is Madame always this busy?'

He betrayed their scant acquaintance, thought Louis. 'Madame? Always.'

'Have you worked for her long?'

'I don't work for Madame: I'm a Ministry employee.'

'Ministry? Which Ministry?'

'I'm a civil servant. I work for the Arts Ministry, as does Madame.'

'Does Madame work for the arts?'

'Madame?' Louis' voice issued from his back, like a living Magritte; it registered a note of ill-concealed and scornful surprise. 'Madame is the director of the Louvre.' This did not make a great impression on R.: he would have been much more intimidated by the news that Polissena had won the Derby.

He knew very little about museums and hardly ever went to them. The Mercedes stopped on one of those streets which intersect the Cromwell Road, and Louis got out without a word. After a few minutes, he returned accompanied by a suitcase and a tall woman. The young woman with curly blonde hair was called Dauphine. She came and sat beside him resolutely. She was conventionally elegant; her shoes and handbag were of brown leather, of traditional design and smell. Everything else was made of tweed, the kind of tweed which the French believe to be English, but which is really far too soft and feminine for English tweed.

She was in the mood for talking.

'I'm Dauphine de Brantes; I've been working for Madame for three years. I'm not French either, as I was born in Switzerland; we all work for France here, though Louis is Belgian, Madame is Spanish and Valentina was born in Latvia, or somewhere like that. We're travelling together to Frankfurt today: Madame has two meetings there. You do know that Madame Braganza has gone before us, don't you? She left for Frankfurt an hour ago. Baron von Wurzburg gave her a lift. He's the greatest art collector in Europe and he's a powerful dealer too. He's someone to be cultivated. Oh! I'm well aware that many of those masterpieces were assembled under the Nazis: they sent their owners off to the ovens and kept their paintings for themselves. But it's wrong to say such things: it's ill-mannered and, who knows? maybe the Baron will leave something to us at the Louvre if we treat him right. You're to meet up tomorrow. Not with the Baron: I mean with Madame. She told me to ask you whether you liked Wagner because she's got two tickets, you lucky things! Just think, most people die before ever seeing a single opera by Wagner performed at Bayreuth . . .'

This verbal onslaught and, in particular, the ideas with which Dauphine was bombarding him caused him some annoyance. Dauphine looked him in the face without any shyness; she took in his square, virile jaw line, the cheek-bones framing his well-formed eyelids and the long lashes shading those eyes which, in the halflight inside the Mercedes, had deepened to a periwinkle blue. 'We're meeting Valentina at the airport. Valentina's been working for Madame for ages. She covers the Eastern side of things: she knows all those languages, including German. As for me, I'm her personal secretary: I know everything about her. I've got the keys to all her flats. I'm her shadow. Valentina's job is organizing dinners, meetings: public relations. Madame's job has become essentially social in character; there's so much to do that we always end up writing the letters which Madame dictates to us at night. I'm not kidding! Sometimes Madame sends us to her dinners in her stead . . .'

He did not like Dauphine; her presumption and her way of talking annoyed him.

R. woke up once they had landed. Dauphine sat next to him whilst Valentina stood by watching him. She had a Slavic surname which he had not properly understood.

But where was Polissena? Why had she left him with her secretaries? Why had she left without him? If she really loved him, as she said she did, she should have waited for him and left with him.

Valentina kept hold of his passport; Dauphine was in charge of the baggage. There was nothing left for R. to do but to watch them passively.

The airport boutiques sold newspapers and magazines, books and salami, loden coats, postcards, feathered Tyrolean hats and Bavarian jackets. Frankfurt airport teemed with money, furs and heavily scented people; it stank of well-being.

He was tired. R. curled up in the car which Valentina had hired from Avis; with her blonde hair tucked into an Hermès scarf, Dauphine was at the wheel. He was not about to ask any more questions. He imagined that they were heading for the centre of Frankfurt, for one of those identikit luxury hotels where he would collapse into a long-coveted sleep. After all, he had not slept much the night before. He felt lost and disappointed. He knew Frankfurt: he knew better than to expect anything other than a vision of cement sparkling with Deutschmarks.

But the car was still making its way along suburban streets when it slowed down and turned into a small garden. Had it not been so shabby with those shrubs trimmed back into small and sinister oblongs, it would have looked like a modern cemetery or a crematorium.

Flicking gravel up against the hedge, the car came to a halt just in front of the main door.

In the hallway, a vast quantity of loden jackets was jumbled together with feathered caps and all those other typically German rustic kitsch artefacts. Horn-made walking-sticks hung from the hall-stand: they had names and edelweiss carved into the knots of the wood. There were also some chains.

'Would you like to sit down?' asked a thin young lady turning from Dauphine to Valentina; then, fixing her gaze steadily on R., she added, 'What type are you after?'

'He doesn't know,' Valentina broke in; 'everything's been ordered by Madame.'

'It's to be a surprise,' Dauphine assured her.

'We'll have to measure him up,' decreed the pale young lady.

'Before joining Madame in Bayreuth,' whispered Dauphine confidentially, looking into R.'s sleepy eyes, 'we have an appointment with this famous firm. It's the Gucci of the market.' Recalling the attendant, she asked, 'Has Madame ordered the two armbands?'

'Yes, those are ready. But the chastity belt for Mr Reading has to be made to measure. We have to try it on.'

'What did you say?' asked R. Up till then, he had not been paying much attention to them: he was tired and wanted nothing more than to get to the hotel and sleep. 'What do you mean by the chastity belt? Those gadgets haven't been in use since the Crusades. Anyway, they're meant only for women, not . . .'

'You're wrong,' interrupted the attendant whose name was Gertrude. 'There are nineteenth-century chastity belts

41

as well as Art Deco chastity belts. People had them made up even under Cromwell.'

'But not any more they don't.'

'You should see our list of clients if that's what you think!' came Gertrude's answer: her friends knew her as Trudi. She was dressed in severe and muddy-coloured woollens. It was as if she wanted to appear older than she actually was, and her thin, drawn skin would certainly prematurely age her. Her hair was pale and thin; it was fastened low on her skull in a pony tail. 'If you wish, you can go and see the museum of chastity belts later on – it takes up the rest of this villa.'

'No, look, I'm not interested in the museum or the belt.'

'What do you mean you're not interested?' Trudi looked at him disapprovingly.

'Madame said you were docile,' murmured Valentina apologetically, 'she said you were submissive.'

'I don't mind the armbands . . . well, I wonder what they really are,' he accepted impatiently, wide awake by this stage.

'They're two metal rings, about two centimetres wide, which you wear on your arms in such a way that your shirt will hide them from view. We'll solder them on tonight.'

'I guess they'll bear my monogram,' said R. ironically, but then he remembered that he found himself in the Ferragamo or Gucci of the slaves' accessories market. This being a fetishist's Hermès, he added, 'Or maybe they'll bear your logo instead.'

'Wrong on both counts. They'll just have a number. But anyone familiar with this kind of product will understand at once where they've come from. It would not be immodest of me to call this the Cartier of the genre.' It was true that Germans were accustomed to giving numbers to their prisoners. But what was his number going to be? What would it mean?

'The chastity belt which Madame ordered for you has been designed by one of our best stylists.'

'What d'you mean "stylists"?' demanded R. He was too worried to be amused.

'We use only the best designers – we too must follow the fashion. You'll also find our boutique not far from the museum you'll be visiting later on. Zips are in this year: it's a bit punk, you know, though such a bore when they get jammed. But, as for yours,' Trudi reassured him, 'Madame has ordered a unique specimen for you: it's made of rubber and precious metals. You have to undress,' she added.

'Where?'

'Here.'

'In front of you?'

'Of course.' Trudi had the manner and the bearing of a nurse who has seen it all before.

'I refuse.'

'Madame assured me that you were more docile,' complained Valentina.

'I don't care what Madame told you.'

'Madame is waiting for you. Madame would be saddened by a refusal,' put in an impassioned Dauphine. 'She says she loves you.'

'But that's another matter. I don't want to take my clothes off in front of her secretaries just because we love one another. Don't let's be ridiculous!'

If only the marchioness his mother could see him now. If only she could imagine where he had ended up! Maybe his mother was right never to abandon the peace and quiet of Monpleasance.

'But we're not here to argue,' said Valentina harshly. 'We're here to ensure that the chastity belt fits like a glove. Come on, get undressed.' She unbuttoned his trousers. 'You don't need to take your jacket off,' she added roughly, in the impatient tone with which you would address a capricious child. Her straightforward approach seemed practised.

'We're only interested in the lower regions,' said Gertrude taking off his shoes and removing his socks.

R. was not wearing underpants since Polissena had ordered him not to.

From a corner of the room decorated by a single painting of two deer at a spring, Gertrude pulled out a small white bed which looked as though it was intended for surgical purposes; she motioned R. to lie down on it. He preferred to imagine himself at the doctor's, but the sight of those three women dominating him from above, watching him as he lay naked from the waist down, humiliated him and excited him at the same time. Their presence was arousing – especially that of Dauphine and Valentina.

'I don't understand how a man can wear a chastity belt,' he said in an effort to break the embarrassed silence which had settled around the small bed. 'If you measure me up now, well, there are physiological changes which occur in men . . . I mean, if I get an erection, the housing made of metal or rubber or whatever it is could damage me.'

'It's just what we're waiting for,' said Trudi. 'We're waiting for you to have an erection because that's what we must fit the chastity belt to.'

Trudi opened a drawer which was divided up into compartments. R. heard the tinkling of metal. 'Let's see, S . . . Simmons, Sodestrom, Siliani, Switzer, no . . . R. Here we are! Reading! Here's yours! Oh! What a lovely belt!' she exclaimed approvingly as she suspended it from her outstretched hands so that they could all admire the handiwork. 'This is one of the very best. You can see that the chain-mail is as fine as on the more antique models; this section fits on the hips, and this is the cap. D'you see? It'll have to be adjusted according to your erection. You'll have to try and get a – how can I put it? – a majestic one, one of your most vigorous.'

'How am I supposed to manage that when you three are watching me like that?' protested R. as he lay supine on his surgical bed.

'You're a young and potent man,' said Gertrude.

'Madame says that you're very potent,' put in Dauphine.

'Madame says you don't have the least difficulty: you only need some touching.'

Indeed Valentina had already started feeling into the corners of his crotch, caressing him delicately and pushing her fingers towards his hotter, softer and more secret recesses.

With horror, R. ascertained that, in spite of himself, his groin was changing shape.

'What about if I took my clothes off?' asked Dauphine with a smile. 'I could rub my body against your budding erection.' She unbuttoned her tweed jacket. She was not wearing any bra.

'Madame would not be pleased by such a display,' protested R. who was upset by the new twist of events. He only had eyes for the large, soft bosom which Dauphine proffered to him, which hung over him, brushing against his abdomen, his shirt, his neck, as Valentina went on feeling his thighs and groin. White and lightly veined, that bosom wanted to be touched and kissed.

'There! Your erection looks almost perfect,' said Valentina contemplating him with satisfaction.

'Maybe just a moment longer.' Trudi began to massage his penis very professionally between both her hands. R. now kept his eyes firmly shut.

'Not too much, else he'll come.'

'Now it's right.'

R. felt that they were fitting a heavy structure to his hips and that his penis was being capped by something. 'It's made of a new metal,' announced Trudi. 'You'll see — you won't have any complaints. In any case, we guarantee our products for two years. This metal is more precious than platinum and it's lighter too. And here's the lock . . .'

He felt the lock click: the mechanism was shutting. 'This lock only has one key and Madame's got it!'

R. opened his eyes. 'How will I manage?'

'Don't worry, Mr Reading: there's a hole,' Trudi informed him affably. She had a heavy German accent. 'One day, a Crusader left on a long journey.' She had obviously started telling her usual joke. 'He shut his wife inside a chastity belt and entrusted the key to his best friend. After a couple of days' march, his friend caught up with him. Breathlessly, he dismounted his horse and, still panting, he cried, "My friend! You gave me the wrong key!" ' Gertrude laughed heartily.

A typically German sense of humour, thought R. But in precisely what kind of trap had he caught himself? 'Anyway, it's not hygienic,' he said.

'There's no reason to think that Madame won't often let you out of it.'

'It's a sophisticated idea,' Dauphine assured him. 'Many important people wear chastity belts, as well as collars, chains, numbered armbands . . .'

'It strikes me as a mere whim,' cut in R. 'When will I see Madame?'

'This evening, or tomorrow.'

VIII

He joined her the following day at Pommersfelden Castle. R. had slept badly thanks to that contraption fixed around his hips; he had been haunted by nightmares featuring Gertrude and small white beds, unwanted surgical operations and Dauphine snipping off his testicles and removing them to the museum to be preserved in ether.

Polissena beamed with pleasure on seeing him; she threw herself into his arms: her mouth was open and her lips were painted brilliant red. 'Dauphine, could you possibly drive us over to Bayreuth this afternoon? . . . Isn't it amazing? We've got two tickets for *Tristan*. Aren't you pleased? It's my favourite Wagner. Which one do you like best?'

'I don't know them at all; I've never heard a single note from any of them.' He was annoyed if not actually angry about all the gear hanging from his hips, chafing beneath the cloth of his trousers. His blue eyes shone opaque; Polissena looked at them and ascertained that R. had not accepted. But he would change within a week. She kissed him on the mouth.

'What are you going to wear this afternoon?'

He was still sulky.

'Dauphine, could you find something, a navy suit or a smart jacket — one of those Bavarian ones. Failing that, you could ask Monsignor Venini to lend us a priest's cassock: they're always extremely smart . . . well, that is if we can find him in the first place.'

'He's always at Pommersfelden at this time of year,' Dauphine reassured her.

'If, instead of having a chastity belt made up for me, you'd measured me up for a suit, then we wouldn't have wasted all this time. I feel it would also have been somewhat more useful. And I'm damned if I'm going to wear a priest's cassock – that's the limit!'

He was really angry, but he was going along with it.

'I went to such trouble to find you that chastity belt,' wailed Polissena in a childish voice: 'you know it's the very best make . . .'

'Stop it! You're teasing me. What exactly do you want from me?'

Polissena squeezed herself against him. Their passion burst out like a flame on petrol.

'Let's go for a walk.'

The mere contact of her hand electrified him. They wandered through Pommersfelden park which had been planted with elms and oaks by the Archbishops, Crown Princes, Electors. The garden was ringed by the forest and extended in a strip before the massive palace.

They went up the rather clumsy baroque grand staircase. Olympian Gods were mounted on the curving balustrade made of roseate marble: a slightly crooked Apollo was frozen in the act of driving his chariot.

'Just look at those chandeliers – how wonderful! Oh! How amusing!' exclaimed Polissena as she wrapped her arm around his. Every now and then, she would flash him a rapid glance, admiring those eyes which, side on, became triangles of bright blue.

He was having fun too: they looked around that rosy gold-tinged world.

'They've got a Collegium Musicum,' she informed him; 'they come every summer to make music together.' She pointed at the closed door at the top of the stairs from which – in highly appropriate fashion – there issued strains of baroque music.

'Who's the Baron who took you to Frankfurt?' he asked.

'Hans-Herbert? A homosexual collector; he might leave us his French pictures . . .'

'Us?'

'The Louvre.'

'You identify yourself with your work.'

'We're the same thing.'

'I'm part of you too, now. But who's to know how many you've played with before me, and tied up in chastity belts and strapped into airplane safety belts?'

'You're the only one,' answered Polissena severely. 'But don't talk like that – you're not to argue: you have to accept.'

'I have to accept. Why is that?'

Sooner or later he would be subjugated, he would submit himself. He was not meant to talk like that, nor even to think of asking her such questions.

'Young people come to Pommersfelden in the summer on scholarships. It's a fantastic place in which to make music together.' She had changed the subject. 'It's such a shame that it should be populated by Germans.'

'Why? What have you got against them?'

'The worst thing about Germans is that they're ugly.' Polissena shook her black curls and her teeth glistened behind her lacquered lips. 'That's why they're so violent.'

The picture collection had not changed since the days of the Bishop Elector of Bamberg and Archbishop of Mainz: the canvases seemed to hang in no particular order, capriciously, close to one another as if arranged merely to fill up the high damask-covered walls. There were some seventeenth-century oval-shaped pictures, fourteenth-century primitives on wood, some fine Flemish landscapes, some copies, and some wonders also.

'It would be hard work cataloguing this collection, but it would be great fun,' said Polissena. She looked at R. In deeply earnest fashion, R. was lingering over one group of canvases, then another. She smiled at him and, in so doing, she reawakened in them both the powerful desire which they felt for one another.

'Monsignor Venini occupies the private apartments, but he's only here for a couple of weeks a year in the summer. He's the Argentinian Legate at the Holy See: would you like to meet him?'

'Me? You must be joking! I want to be alone with you!'

'He's a queer fish, is Ermenegildo. He's very powerful: a kind of Licio Gelli figure. But P2 is peanuts to him: he's got P3, P4 and P5 tucked up his sleeve; like all Argentinians, he's half mafioso and half Nazi. You do know that all the mafia and the Nazi bosses fled to Argentina and had their faces changed over there, don't you? Not that they needed plastic surgery, seeing as the more mafioso and Nazi you are in South America, the happier they are to have you.'

'So how do you know him?'

'Monsignor Venini? Well, I don't really.'

Under the stairway was a small door, concealed by an ornate vault studded with seashells and mother-of-pearl. Polissena pushed it open with a familiar touch. 'This is such a delightful room!' she said, laughing. 'It's where the Bishop Electors used to get up to every conceivable kind of wickedness.' She clearly found the idea exciting. 'Orgies: just think! Try and imagine!'

She shut the door behind her.

'They cavorted about these niches, do you see? They're all made of mother-of-pearl and violet mussel shells, and the candelabra are shaped like fish. They must have twinkled in the gloom; the small tongues of flame would have been mirrored in the hearts of these shells. Imagine seeing these statues of Nereids and of Neptune trembling and shuddering in the candlelight. Down there were fountains and jets of water which glittered as the stream flowed and unravelled its course in the fountains outside, in the garden out there. It must have been like Versailles out there with all those statues and fountains . . . then along came the vogue for English gardens and so they destroyed all the terracing, and the cisterns and fountains, and turned everything into lawns and parkland. What idiots!' R. hung on her words: he was enchanted. He loved to hear her talk, to listen to her telling him all those things.

Polissena met his gaze. She wore a small chain around her neck: a glinting key dangled from it.

'Will you free me?'

'I'll free you.'

'And what do the numbers on the armbands stand for? 88: does that mean I'm your 88th conquest?'

'One day you'll understand. But not yet.'

Over on the right was a trompe l'oeil recess in which a powerful-looking Samson was destroying the Temple.

The painter had employed all his artifice to convey the impression that the collapse of the columns was both imminent and terrifying. But he had not quite succeeded in matching the quality of Guido Reni's work in the Casa Tè, which was clearly the vision that had inspired those images.

'Let's open the windows,' said R. 'Look! There are musicians out there as well!'

'When I was little, I learnt to play the cello.'

It was a peculiar revelation; he would never have guessed that Polissena had played on such a massive instrument.

As she stood beside the rococo arches, her scarlet mouth had begun to hum a Mozartian ditty; her black curls were tossed by the breeze which blew in from the park; she looked as though she was muttering to herself.

Suddenly she sprang towards him.

'Quick! Let's get undressed!'

'You must be crazy! What about all those people outside? All those boys and girls making music out there in the park: they might see us. I mean, we're in a public place, a museum. A bunch of tourists could turn up . . . Let's go to your room instead.'

'It's much more fun out here: I enjoy the risk, the likelihood of being found out.'

'I couldn't possibly manage it . . . and you'd have to take off my chastity belt in any case.'

She unbuttoned his shirt and fingered his steel armbands which were fastened above the elbow. She undid his trousers. She bent down without removing the key from the chain from which it was suspended and undid the lock which shut him in.

'You see,' said Polissena as she touched his sex and licked the soft tip, grazing it with her fingers. 'Can't you see that you want it?'

'I always want it when you touch me. You have the most incredible effect on me.'

'You do too,' she countered earnestly as she knelt over him. 'But it's uncomfortable on the floor.' His hand slid under her skirt: neither of them was wearing any pants.

'I'm ready too.' R. applied all his strength as he pushed his body into the wet opening proffered to him. The muscles of his thighs wrapped themselves around the violence contained within her hot recess and relayed his momentum into her. Her whole body was charged with his warmth. He could feel Polissena's bosom squashed against his chest; their tongues twisted and turned together, tormenting and penetrating each other.

Polissena's hands were on his head; her fingers ran through his chestnut curls, into his small ears and his nostrils. Then R. emptied his belly inside her, filling her with the waves of his orgasms.

'You see, you did come!' she said triumphantly.

'I think the musicians must have seen us.'

'The music was meant for us. Music and making love come to the same thing, especially in Wagner's case. Wagner's just like an extended orgasm: a slow, protracted masturbation, during which the same movements are repeated over and over again.' They got up.

'Next time, I want to make love on top of you. I want to imagine myself in the man's place, as if it was me who was taking you.'

'You'd better choose a less uncomfortable floor then. But please don't ask me to put that belt back on . . .'

'Stuff it into your pocket: you'll have to wear it when I punish you.'

'And why will you have to punish me?'

'Oh! I'll have to punish you often because that's the way it has to be.'

They got to Bayreuth at three. The performance began at four.

IX

The Bayreuth auditorium reverberated like a violin: the whole theatre was indeed constructed of wood. From the beginning, when the first notes sounded of the opera with which R. was totally unfamiliar, his spine reacted to the music with tiny spasms which tingled in his stomach and stirred him into shedding irrational tears. The orchestra played magnificently under the direction of the younger Daniel Barenboim. Goodness only knew what that tiny Jew felt as he conducted from the core of the mystic canon which had inspired so much pan-Germanism, so much hatred and so much Nazi rhetoric.

One half of the audience which filled the auditorium was made up of Jews, the other half by former SS officers. So Baron von Wurzburg had decreed. Looking around, R. had added, 'And homosexuals too,' without realizing that, in spite of his seventy years, the Baron was still an active member of the subgroup.

'Come to that, there's also a fair sprinkling of Japanese,' chipped in Milagros Gautier, a famous antiques dealer who had made the journey from Munich especially to see *Tristan*.

'. . . as well as music directors, agents and artistic directors,' added Vladislav Huk, who belonged to this last category and had just joined the little group.

'Vladislav is the artistic director of the Bratislava Theatre,' explained Polissena, guiding R.'s eyes to the tall and ascetically thin figure standing beside them; his hair was precociously white and his face precociously hostile.

'You should get the Till Theatre in Prague,' the Baron suggested to Vladislav; 'you could put on a whole load of baroque operas.'

'It's still shut. We're rearranging it – they're tarting it up. They've painted all those buildings which have any association with Mozart. If you go back to Prague, you almost can't recognize it any more; they've glossed over all that Kafkaesque greyness in pretty-pretty gold.'

'That's just it,' said Milagros Gautier despondently; she was an ancient lady who travelled continuously, knew everything and who, in defiance of her eighty years, never failed to go swimming in Capri every March before Easter.

'What a good idea! Let's go to Prague!' exclaimed Polissena, with that sombre look which her dark eyes set in the pallor of her face always gave her. As usual, her mouth was garishly painted and matched the freesia hues of a long dress which hugged her slim waist, though it did not suit her.

'You'll see how beautiful Prague's Malastrana is: those palaces . . .' she went on, turning to R. who had not the slightest intention of going to Prague.

'Unfortunately you have to accept the new chocolate-box Prague, but on the inside, and in spirit, it's still grey. The pink gloss is just for films – Prague's become a permanent film set for eighteenth-century yarns, or for documentaries on the Prague Spring; it's the Slav version of Hollywood.'

'You can't complain, Vladislav. The Till is still the only theatre for *Don Giovanni*, the greatest opera ever written,' said Milagros. 'And when they reopen it, I'll be off there like a shot.'

'What? For a *Don Giovanni* that's probably shoddily done?' interrupted the Baron, who was an irrepressible Wagner enthusiast. In his books, there was no music to match Wagner but then, that is the way it goes: Wagner is totalitarian. 'Better still, we should go to Prague for the interesting things you can buy there.'

'In Prague?' queried Polissena: she was intrigued.

'Well, it is risky,' commented Milagros as she bit into a wurst smothered in yellow mustard.

'How do you export anything out of Czechoslovakia? What kind of thing are we talking about anyway?'

'Drawings by Dürer . . . I heard about a Caravaggio, a real one: Monsignor Venini assured me that it's outstanding. My dream is to own a Caravaggio! I don't have a single one and the Polignac-Hérissons have all of two: d'you see my point? Two . . .' It was clearly a very sore point. R. looked at him in surprise and took the glass of champagne which the Baron tendered him. He had ordered it for all of them without any of them noticing.

'If it's a genuine Caravaggio,' mused Polissena, 'then it must have been stolen.'

R. felt left out. The interval was an hour long. He saw people talking into mobile telephones which they fished out of their dinner-jacket pockets; they were dictating to their offices, adding to the wealth of West Germany.

'What are you doing here, my boy?' Lady Isabella brushed her pale English cheek against R.'s lips. She kissed into the air, ruling out intimate contact with her son. The presence of the Marchioness of Beckford at Bayreuth was just as improbable as that of her son. Stunned by surprise, R. asked her, 'Do you really like Wagner?'

'Who? My dear boy, I'm so absent-minded, I never remember the names – oh! but I do love music, all of it. I'm really very musical: everyone's always told me so.'

How could he prevent his mother from realizing that he was at Bayreuth in the company of Cousin Polissena Lockhart? Luckily, Polissena was half hidden by the group which had drifted towards the bar some way away. His mother would not have asked any questions in any case; it was not so much a matter of good manners as because she was profoundly uninterested in what her own children got up to.

'But you're . . .'

'I'm here with Cousin Charles. He invited me at the very last moment. Tomorrow morning we're going to the Saxe-Coburgs with the Prince of Wales.'

'The old girl thought we were in Salzburg until the curtain went up,' confided Cousin Charles; 'but in Salzburg, the acts wouldn't last so damnably long and the audience would be rather more elegant.'

'Too right; that first act was interminable,' the marchioness broke in. She was surprised to catch sight of Polissena who had approached them in the meantime. Lady Isabella stared at her. 'Cousin, what are you doing here?' Since the answer was not of any interest to her, she moved on to the introductions, 'Cousin Charles, Cousin Polissena . . .'

'Vladislav Huk.'

'Marian Svoboda of the Prague State Museum,' a young man with a thick moustache was introducing himself; he had fallen in behind Vladislav and Milagros.

'The Duke of Soho, my cousin,' countered Lady Isabella.

'The Marchioness Beckford,' Cousin Charles responded,

'my cousin and . . . her son.' He thus indicated R.: his name had momentarily escaped him.

Amidst the serving bars and the queues of hopeful enthusiasts yearning to find tickets, holding up placards on which were written the words '*Suche Karte*', between the vast German ladies dressed in pink and the obese forms of sullen-faced husbands with porcine chins, Nicholas Newman swam into view. 'Me? How could I miss out on such a *Tristan*? Never! Eh? It's time, isn't it? Am I right or am I right? Mr Reading, what a pleasant surprise! And here's Polissena and Marian. Well, well, all the museums are here, along with the Baron who's almost a museum in his own right, I mean, his collection, eh? How is the Baron?'

R. and Polissena exchanged a long look of conspiratorial passion. That bright blue seemed to swathe her.

Out broke the second act: it was a cry of voluptuousness. No other composer has ever described the passionate emotion with such accuracy.

X

It was a peculiar place to choose for their post-performance entertainment, thought R. as he peered through the darkness into the deserted villa in the middle of the Hofgarten. The Baron was with them, together with the two Czechs, Marian and Vladislav. Dauphine had materialized outside

60

the opera house with the car and it was she who had driven them to the Hofgarten on the other side of Bayreuth.

'It was fantastic,' Polissena cut short the enquiry. Accounts of performances, like those about travels, were always extremely dull for those who had not taken part.

They walked through a side gate under the dripping rain; the group was received by the curator at the entrance to the villa.

This was because Wahnfried, the Haven of Rest, was also a museum. 'Cosima and Richard Wagner lived here,' Vladislav explained to R. who was the only one present to be unaware of the fact. 'Cosima, Cosima Liszt, the second wife, Liszt's daughter.'

'Liszt was a composer who screwed out of snobbery: that's why his daughter was so ugly,' exclaimed the Baron, who had no taste for women, be they duchesses or chambermaids.

They crossed the entrance-hall which was covered in a frescoed frieze depicting the Epic of the Ring of the Nibelungs. Along it ran a gallery. Then they came to a huge empty room, devoid of furniture except for the bookcases and the piano which stood near the window giving on to the dark rainy garden.

'Don't switch the lights on,' warned the curator as he struck a match. 'We shouldn't be here: I wouldn't want anyone to notice that the lights were on, even if no one's ever around usually: the park is closed at night.'

A couple of flickering candles lent the atmosphere a funereal air.

'This house was designed by Wagner himself,' Polissena told R. It was a strange mixture of the genteel and the grandiose.

All of a sudden the room was invaded by the strains of Wagnerian music. Siegfried, in a recording dating back to the forties, was sailing down the Rhine.

'This was Wagner's drawing room,' explained the curator. 'Once it held a library of 2,310 books! If only it wasn't raining and it wasn't quite so dark, we'd be able to see the tomb of the composer and his wife from the windows. All that was in this room was specially made for Wagner: tables, chairs, bookshelves, all designed by a Munich sculptor called Lorenz Gedon. But in 1945 a bomb dropped on the villa and completely destroyed this room: all the furniture and the books were incinerated.'

The Allies' bomb had certainly hit the bull's-eye; it had found its way into the heart of Nazism.

R. made no comment, principally because he had nothing to say and also because he was disappointed. He would have liked to spend that night alone with Polissena. Instead of which, great dishes piled with smoked meats and large quantities of aquavit were brought out. Meanwhile, Brunhilde was preparing to immolate herself upon Siegfried's pyre – just like an Indian widow – without even sparing her thoroughbred: a real waste, reflected R. who was fond of horses.

'Now we're going to play a game,' announced Baron von Wurzburg. His pale face beamed with an angelic smile. Polissena felt a stab of pleasure as she intuited that R. was to be the victim of this game.

'Let's deal out the cards,' suggested Vladislav with a pack ready in his hand. It all looked like part of some pre-established programme, especially when the gloved hand stopped at R. The periwinkle eyes looked quizzically at the Baron and then moved on to Polissena. She smiled at him and kissed him on the mouth in front of everyone. Taking him by the hand, she beckoned, 'Come!' She placed a thick black headband around his temples and fastened a tight knot. 'Can you see?'

'No.'

'Sure?'

'Sure.'

They went outside; she led him, and the others walked just behind them. The arch of Polissena's palm enfolded his hand as they walked on in silence. R. was rather drunk on aquavit. It was not raining any more.

He could hear their quiet whispering and the crunch of their footsteps on the gravel behind him; he heard the elms rustling in the breeze.

'How does this game go?' R. asked Polissena. She made him stop for a moment and gave him another slug of aquavit to drink from the bottle which she was holding in her other hand. Then she kissed him on the mouth again.

As they were still burning from their contact with alcohol, R.'s lips were taken by other lips. 'Whose are these? Are they yours?' asked R. in despair. He had heard low footsteps. He could sense that the others were near them both, nearer than before. 'Was it you?'

'Guess!' answered a voice which might have been Dauphine's.

But he was unable to guess; he was drunk and beginning to feel the cold; that music which kept coming out in waves from the veranda of Wahnfried intoxicated him; it almost made him nauseous. And he was ashamed at his inability to distinguish the kisses: was Polissena the one who had taken him with her lips? Or was it somebody else?

This time the kiss was so much more violent that R. lost his balance and fell on to a slab of cold stone; he could sense the others' presence close by. 'Who was that?'

'You tell us – you guess!' answered Marian.

'Guess!' insisted the curator's voice.

He suspected that they were all in this together, Polissena included. The game was some kind of conspiracy. But then he recognized her touch: Polissena's hands were sliding down his back, feeling their way down the folds of his trousers. He was supine on the cold stone.

'Relax,' she murmured invitingly. 'Now I've got to punish you for failing to recognize my kisses from those of the others.'

He felt her taking off his trousers; other hands were helping her. Now somebody had taken his sex in their mouth, but it could not be Polissena because he could feel her presence beside him, kissing his ears which were partly covered by the headband, and kissing his mouth. But was it really Polissena who was kissing him? Maybe it was someone else pretending to be her?

'Who was it who just kissed you?' She got up on her feet, shifting away from him. 'We've got to punish you.'

She pushed him hard and he rolled over on to his side.

'I'll fall.'

'Don't worry – it's a large slab.'

'What is?'

R. would never have suspected that he was lying prone on top of the double tomb of Cosima and Richard Wagner. Two people held down his arms from above, and another leant on the edge of the cold stone and bent over him, prising apart his buttocks and opening up a passage for himself. 'No! Not this! I don't want to . . . Polissena, I don't want to!'

'Do it for me: obey,' Polissena's voice coaxed gently by his ears. A hot pulsating penis was thrusting against him.

'He's hermetically sealed,' complained a male voice, maybe Marian's. 'Someone's got to help me – keep his buttocks apart!'

His pain was lacerating. The more he cried out, the more the strains of *Parsifal* smothered his lamentations.

'Don't cry out,' murmured her voice; 'imagine it's me that's penetrating you – it's as though I were taking you.' As that throbbing object pierced ever more deeply into his flesh, R. went on screaming. He could feel him pressing on his guts, he could feel him rising up and pushing down on top of him, pushing right up to his brain. Then the man who was raping him burst into sobs and everyone clapped their hands whilst R. wept tears of pain and panic and humiliation.

'Now I'll have him,' said another voice, maybe the Baron's.

'No!' countered Polissena: 'That's enough.'

On hearing her voice, R. felt the grip on his arms loosening and leaving him; he heard footsteps moving away and felt her hands seeking him. When she removed his headband, he realized they had been left on their own; a candelabrum dripped with wax in the wind.

'Darling,' she said, 'I will comfort you now.'

XI

It had been raining for four hours when they got to the border crossing at Schirnding. R. had spent years dissecting racing cars and could hardly restrain his vexation at being a passenger in a car driven by a woman. As it was, Polissena drove without any particular attention or flair; to her, driving was a purely functional activity, not a special ability.

Having passed through German customs, marked out merely by two guards and a petrol pump, they crossed into Czech territory which, up to 1945, had been German. Now the barbed wire threaded along the frontier, up into the hills and along the minefields and the closed-off border crossings, past the yapping dogs and the soldiers armed with sub-machine-guns – all that wire served as a vivid reminder of the extermination camps set up by the country which had invaded them back in 1938.

'The only advantage of travelling to these countries run by dictatorial regimes is that, being so uninviting, they discourage most tourists,' opined Polissena.

It was raining.

They waited around for two hours whilst their various papers, the two passports and the documents relating to the car were all carefully examined by the young Czech guards with their blue uniforms and angular features. They were better-looking than Germans, reflected Polissena, but they were neither one thing nor another, neither German nor Slav, though they wanted to be more German than the Germans. Like all hybrid countries, they were fiercely patriotic. Their music spoke of the Czech mountains and rivers, of Ma Vlast and the homeland; those born in Moravia considered Slovenia to be as remote as another planet, and viewed Slovaks as enemies. Bohemia was a different world altogether.

'You're not angry.' Polissena's was not a query: it was a statement of fact. R. knew what she was referring to. Yes, he was still smarting.

He did not respond.

'You're going to a place which you'll find interesting. It will educate you, and change you,' she added. 'You'll go through with it because you love me and, afterwards, you'll love me still more. Anyway, you'd do anything for me.'

How was it possible to say such things in that almost hypnotic tone? How could he really believe what she told him? He decided not to make any comment; there was admittedly some truth in what she said. He wanted to obey her in order to oblige her and to give her pleasure. 'I've never been here before,' R. broke the silence and interrupted her thoughts. He looked sleepily at the rain beating down on the windscreen and slipping down the windows. He was beginning to worry that Polissena might abandon him. That night, he even woke up with a start in a cold sweat thinking that she had taken off, that she had found something better. He was in despair.

'I come here every so often. That's why they take so long with my passport: they get suspicious. They don't really want any tourists, but now they need foreign exchange.'

'Do they check up on you?'

'Maybe – it's common practice in the Balkans.' Polissena smeared another layer of lipstick on her lips; the raindrops drummed on the awning covering the roadblock.

'We'll have to change something at the frontier.'

'What do you mean?' she asked.

'Our money.' R. had a few dollars and pounds and changed them all.

'That was silly,' Polissena rebuked him. 'You could have got twice as much on the black market.'

'But that's forbidden . . . and I didn't have much money to change anyway.'

'You won't need any.'

They were driving again; the landscape had not changed much. What was Polissena saying? He wanted to take her out to dinner, they had been told that the restaurants in Prague were quaint and sophisticated, that one ate well. It was raining.

There were still three roadblocks to negotiate. Polissena seemed used to it; she stuck a hand out of the window, flashing the pass which she had been handed at the frontier. 'But why do you come here?' insisted R.

In the rain, the shapes of the Hanseatic church steeples dissolved on the windows of the car.

She explained that there were still some important pictures to be found in Czechoslovakia; that some great collections had been built up here in the days of the Austro-Hungarian Empire; that, in any case, she felt a kind of secret pleasure in suspecting the presence of microphones in every hotel, along with strange ears tapped into each telephone. She did not know why, but that was her way; it gratified her to encounter such obstacles.

It was still raining.

'Listen,' she said to him as she looked ahead into the rain; 'we're not going to Prague right away, but to Ceské Budějovice and I'll be leaving you at the castle. I'll come and pick you up in a week's time.'

R. looked at her in astonishment, unable to put up any protest.

She told him that his numbered armbands would serve as his passport.

'Are you leaving me?' he asked, a quiver of panic in his voice.

'No, no: on the contrary. It's so that I never leave you, ever.'

She asked him to do up his chastity belt once again. She would surrender its key to the castle.

'Which castle?'

R. would go along with it for love of her; if he really

was hers, R. had to accept everything that was demanded of him.

For her part, Polissena reassured him: she had never loved as she did then. She loved him passionately, she loved him with dedication.

XII

They had passed through woods and countryside which undulated under the rain. Polissena drove the car along avenues which twisted back on themselves, around marble statues of goddesses grown over with moss; they had arrived – they were in the grounds of the castle.

The boughs of the gigantic trees hung low, their leaves sodden with glistening rain. The great beeches rustled. It was still raining.

At last, through the branches, R. picked out the topmost turret of Hloboke nad Vltatov.

'What time are they expecting us?' he asked.

'They're only expecting you.'

'Am I to go there alone?'

'Yes, alone.'

'Why?'

'You've got to do it for my sake. I'll be coming back to collect you in a week's time.'

'Why?'

'Because I want you docile, compliant.'

'Why?'

'So that I can love you always. But you have to want it too; you must force yourself – you have to if you love me.'

R. flung himself on her lap and kissed her bare knees, just edged by her velvet skirt.

'You'll be taught new things at the castle. You'll be shown a new way of being and of loving – the satisfaction of not reacting, of being a slave: my slave. Everything they'll do to you, you must submit to for my sake.'

'But you're not coming in with me? Aren't you even going to introduce me?'

They had reached the gravel expanse in front of the massive castle with its gothic crenellations. Polissena stopped the car before the castle which had once belonged to the Hradec family and had then been passed on – like almost everything else – to the Schwarzenbergs.

He looked at it as if lost.

'Now go.' She would come and visit him, she told him, but only as a guest of the castle, a member; he might not even recognize her.

R. made as if to get his suitcase.

'No, you won't need that.'

On the back seat lay his leather shoulder-bag with his books, newspapers, documents. 'You won't need that here either.'

Polissena had been holding down the clutch pedal. Now she let the car go and drove away slowly under the rain as R. stood watching her.

Once alone, R. walked slowly towards the great door

of Hloboke. There was no doorbell or knocker so he decided to push the heavy door. It gave way noisily and let him in.

It was dark but well-heated inside the hall. The walls were painted Pompeian red and adorned with the antlers of deer and *schvec*, the wild goat native to Bohemia; it was lined with the various violent trophies of the chase. Bewildered, he stopped in the middle of the lobby, not knowing what to do next. Whyever had he landed himself in this mess? Because he loved her and wanted to be hers. But if he just thought of how far away he was from home in a country he did not know, where he did not speak the language, and lacked both money and papers, he was seized by panic and despair.

No, he had to trust in her. She was putting him to the test and he would submit for her sake, because he had promised that he would, because he wanted to be hers for ever – he wanted to be her object.

But why was it that Polissena wanted to reduce him to an object? It was her way of loving and in him she had found someone almost totally acquiescent. He himself had discovered a new kind of freedom, of joy and liberation in that newly discovered sensuality; through servility he found sexual redemption. It seemed to him that his being raped in public the previous day had won him over, and now he was ready to undergo any form of humiliation.

It was one way of being free – though he could feel his bond to Polissena grow ever stronger. He could see that it was a bond which she wanted to mould to her own specifications.

Suddenly R. heard a door being opened behind him

and he saw two young women coming towards him. They were both pretty and petite and wore a strange costume. It was an ample cloak made of some rigid fabric, the collar of which rose and flared around their hair, covering up their bodies completely. But when they walked, their legs drew the covering aside, revealing part of their bosom, as well as the belly and the mons veneris. He wondered whether he had not stepped into a brothel, but the two did not allow him to think on such lines for long: without a word, they invited him to follow them. R. walked through various rooms; each was progressively smaller and hotter. The summer heating struck him as excessive.

Every room was painted in dark nineteenth-century tones; hanging from the walls were canvases depicting patriotic deeds, bloody martyrdoms and stormy seas. The furniture was ponderous: he passed some phoney medieval antiques, some dark carved oak panels and ebony reliefs. Dusty, heavy curtains lined whole walls and dark tapestries disappeared into the gloom of the vast hall.

The attendants motioned for him to follow them and, brushing aside a crimson damask curtain, he stepped into an environment which could not have contrasted more markedly with the heavy decoration of the atrium and lobby. This room was altogether white, with aluminium lights of modern design, a bench of undulating marble and a small table made of brass and steel. Some music, which rose in an increasingly deafening crescendo, had suddenly come on, exploding around him in hostile and aggressive noises. It seemed to claw at him.

The heating, which seemed stuck on its winter setting,

was all the more suffocating to this Englishman brought up to live in rigorously cold climes within the uncomfortable rooms of his various homes; he felt his immediate discomfort keenly.

Suddenly he noticed a horrible-looking man in a darker corner of the room. Aside from his long red goatskin gloves and the leather belt around his waist, the man had nothing on. Whips and lashes and a cat-o'-nine-tails hung from his belt, together with some riding crops, and these bunched around his sides and virtually dressed him, thus forming an absurd type of skirt.

R. felt faint at the sight of him; he lost consciousness.

PART TWO

I

His two attendants were called Eva and Sona; they asked him what his number was. Since R. was still lying in a daze on the floor, they felt his armbands and read off his number: '88' was to be his name. What's more, the number determined the type of treatment which he was to undergo within the walls of Hloboke.

The valet with the red gloves and the menacing belt whose name, explained Eva and Sona, was Lubomir Zizka, had vanished by this stage.

Swathed in the capes which left their breasts and stomach bare as they moved, the two attendants preceded him into a small room fitted out in creamy beige wall-to-wall carpeting; it was very thick, shaggy and soft: the same music which had caused him to faint reverberated around the walls. They undressed him and left him wearing his armbands and chastity belt; the belt was to be removed that evening, they informed him.

They immersed him in a jacuzzi which bubbled with mineral water. 88 had not at first noticed it as it was concealed by the shaggy pile of the carpet. Like something out of Alma Tadema, two steps of white marble led down to a large bath. In order to wash him, the two attendants removed their cloaks and were thus left utterly naked. They insisted on lathering and rinsing his body. Squatting on the marble edge with their knees apart, Eva and Sona showed off the full lips of their lower bellies, which were offered up and completely exposed. Their pink and scarlet secrets stretched with their every movement and, as they scrubbed 88's back, bending their white arms towards the bath, their rosy breasts tilted up towards him. They got up on their feet and, as if performing some ritual, they scattered jasmine blossoms and perfumed essences into the warm and bubbling water of the bath.

After about an hour they made him get up and dried him with thick warm towels which had been specially heated for him and which all bore his number: 88. They then made him lie down on a bed where he was massaged with almond oil mixed with an extract of tuberose.

They touched him with professional expertise and in total silence – they did not even talk between themselves. They sprinkled rosewater on the soles of his feet, into the folds of his thighs and under his armpits. Then they turned him over like a fish and performed a treatment specially suited to the nape of the neck which let them linger on his face. Massaging lightly with their expert fingers, Eva and Sona revived the tissue around his blue eyes, above his deep and finely traced eyelids, around his narrow nostrils, and his thin, small, sharp and silent lips. Using the palm of her hand, Eva smoothed his temples, and then applied pressure on the nasal septum with such delicacy and skill that R. fell asleep.

When he reopened his eyes some twenty minutes later, Eva and Sona were in the room; those cloaks of stiff stuff which they had put on once more seemed to fill up most of the room, creating triangular shapes like fir trees, reminiscent of the Madonna of Loreto.

Holding up a flask which could have been made of glass or crystal, Sona poured out some pungent perfume on to one hand and then rubbed it against the other. Then she slid her hands into his groin, covering the curly hairs around his chastity belt with perfume and rubbing it into his armpits and behind his ears also.

He was told he was to eat alone, but that he would be introduced that evening. He was to be assisted by the two attendants Sona Schepflogove and Eva Rybara, and he would be meeting Morella Pallenberg, the chief attendant, and Lubomir Zizka, the valet whom he had glimpsed beforehand. Lubomir spoke only Czech so it was pointless trying to communicate with him.

They did not dress him again. He remained naked, wearing only his armbands and the chastity belt. He wore nothing on his feet. They then escorted him into a second room which was also painted white, and also decorated in ultra-modern style and where the music persisted in wounding him. One of the walls consisted of a huge mirror which reached up to the ceiling.

Two more girls dressed in the same way as Eva and Sona attended to his hands and feet. He wondered whether these were not in fact the same girls as before as they looked so much alike, but they were obviously selected according to the same criteria: height, size and colouring.

Besides, those vast stiff cloaks which flounced about as the girls walked or sat down rendered them alike in their movements also. R. had eyes only for their smooth breasts and polished thighs which merged into that dark central triangle. Though they were small in build, these serving wenches possessed striking lineaments – large eyes devoid of any spark of liveliness, and even their voices lacked intonation when they spoke. Their words were mere sounds.

One of the original wenches returned. It could have been Eva. She indicated that she was going to wash his hair. They brought in a barber's kit, one of those old-fashioned ones of polished brass and enamel. The attendant who had addressed him (maybe it was Sona after all) shampooed his scalp with highly scented balsam. These sweet, exotic and penetrating smells were quite alien to a man like R., used as he was to country living, to cold rooms and the luxurious discomfort peculiar to the Anglo-Saxon male existence.

Sitting in the barber's chair with his legs apart, he examined himself with some embarrassment, taking in the strong arms mirrored before him, and the core of his forsaken groin, now looking almost pathetic. He was told that as 88, he was neither to complain nor was he at liberty to make any choices, that he was to accept whatever was done to him. He was to spend most of the day in his cell, sometimes in the company of his valet Lubomir, sometimes with Morella, whom he had not yet had occasion to meet. He was to spend the evenings with the castle guests; then he would sometimes be blindfolded so that he would be unable to recognize them; at other times, the guests themselves would be masked. Often his lover would take part in these evening entertainments. As Madame was a member of the Club, she would intervene regularly in these evening encounters in which men would participate also. During the night, 88 would often be woken by his valet or his wench and he was not to protest. They would sometimes keep him tied up for a while, suspended from the armbands which he had been wearing ever since he went to Frankfurt, and it would then be forbidden for him to doze off again. But he would be able to rest in the morning until midday or one o'clock at which point he would go for a walk in the park before breakfast.

That evening, when he was finally ready, exhausted and scented, the two wenches escorted him to a third room similar to the one in which he had taken a bath and been massaged.

Lubomir came back. 88 had glimpsed him a few minutes beforehand. He carried a measuring tape and a notepad in his hand. The pencil lay on a small Lalique tray. 88 was told that they would measure his neck to forge him a collar and also some manacles.

The room in which he was to dine was lit up by two dim lamps borne by angels which looked fit for a cemetery. He would not have been able to read books or newspapers in such suffused light even if this diversion had been allowed him, but 88 had the distinct impression that this too was forbidden by the house rules of Hloboke nad Vltatov. Indeed, the room was drowned in shadows and there was not a book in sight. It was a funnel-shaped space and the wide steps which were covered in thick carpet formed a kind of upturned mastaba.

The carpet not only covered the floor and the wide steps, it also blanketed the ceiling. It gave the room a claustrophobic feel: 88 felt suffocated. The room was all white. There were no windows apart from a hatch framed in brass which was opened now and then; through it were passed the delicate dishes for his dinner. Tired and famished, 88 reclined and began to consume the soufflés offered to him. They were magnificently presented, garnished with fresh watercress and artichoke hearts. There were freshwater crabs perched on a delicate mousseline, carp stuffed with snipe and served with fruity Moravian wine, and a succulent steak of *schvec* meat with a sauce of juniper berries. 88 would have preferred to drink beer to quench his thirst. After all, Czechoslovakia was renowned for the excellence of its brews. But there was no one to communicate with, from whom to order anything or make any request. Obviously – 88 had taken in this much – he had no right to demand anything in that castle.

He was there to learn and accept.

II

He stayed in that darkened room for a long time. He could not tell exactly how long, as they had not left him his watch and he could not tell whether it was day or night because there were no windows in that strange, soft and stifling room.

With his hands resting on his knees, 88 remained seated for at least two hours, trying to avoid thinking about the slow passage of time, and also trying not to anticipate what lay in store for him. Then he lay down on one of the steps which doubled up as a bed; he could smell the various fragrant aromas emanating from his own body, and he touched his skin which had been smoothed by so many ointments, lotions and massages.

More long minutes ticked by.

The door burst open at last and the two serving wenches came in followed by Morella.

Morella Pallenberg was tall, with blonde wavy hair cascading down in a magnificent mane about her face and neck; her cold eyes were splendidly framed by long lashes thickened with green mascara. She wore a costume like Batgirl and her legs seemed lengthened by her blue body-stocking and the shiny black belt which hung loose around her waist. She would instruct him, he was told: 88 would obey her in all things. Morella had an authoritarian manner and bore her head high. Sona Schepflogove and Eva Rybara took their orders from her and they would rule him with a rod of iron. Clasping two steel fetters in her hand, Morella fastened them to 88's ankles. These too were imprinted with his number, as was his new collar. Having ascertained that it fitted without pinching his neck, the lock was made to click home with a relentless and menacing clang. All three metal bands had small rings attached; from these they were able to hang him from the walls or suspend him from the ceiling as Morella, his chief attendant, told him. This time, they were going to connect his feet with a fine chain which was not so short that it would trip him up. This fine chain would hardly ever be removed.

Eva and Sona had already bound his hands behind his back using the armbands which Polissena had given him in Frankfurt. The serving wenches went on surveying him with critical detachment. They combed him and sprayed further scented extracts on his smooth skin; then they gently brushed the curls of his groin, and applied make-up, smudging his eyelids with eyeshadow and delicately painting the tip of his penis with some light-coloured lipstick.

Eventually Morella motioned for him to follow her.

They chaperoned him through a series of rooms. The first few were overheated and similar to the one he had just left; they were all lined with thick carpet and very clean; these too had no windows. The little band emerged into that wing of Hloboke which was constructed of gothic vaults; the ochre stone was chipped and aged, the windows narrow, the chairs high and the tapestries vast. Every fire-place spat out great sparks and incandescent embers. In a second great chamber, huge eighteenth-century candelabra hung from the ceiling, as did six or seven glass cages. The cages were spacious and the glass sparkled; each one of them was occupied by a man whose every feature was visible to 88, as the base of each cage was also of transparent glass. The strange furniture glittered in the light of the little flames mounted on the candelabra; as well as the young men who did not appear to be particularly desperate about their bizarre confinement, the cages also contained white lilies and tuberoses: their pungence overwhelmed him.

When he stepped into a smaller room, the walls of which were covered in crimson silk damask, he spotted a great gothic window which gave on to the dark garden; the inky rain drummed against the window panes and ran down the glass outside. A colonnade divided a library decked out in worn-out leather from a dining area. In here, five people were sitting around the table. They had just finished eating: they were unrecognizable beneath their masks. The white expressionless mask emerged from a mantle which was made of brown iridescent silk; the hood crumpled around the face in a ruff which hid from view even the mouth of the wearer. 88 could not therefore work out whether the five were all women or whether he found himself in mixed company. But when he was freed from the chastity belt with the little key he knew so well, he realized that those gloved hands had to belong to Polissena. But could they not have belonged to somebody else? After all, Polissena had handed over the key to the Club, to the castle. However, before long, he was able to recognize her voice as she boasted to the others about his physical attributes: he was young, with unblemished skin; he was strong and highly sexed. He could come six or seven times in one night. The gloved hands took hold of his penis to show him off to the other masked figures; one of these squeezed his testicles and, from the rear, stuck two fingers up his tight and secret passage with such force as to cause him to cry out in pain. But his hands were tied behind his back and his feet were prisoners of one another.

'Let's have a look at him from behind,' said one of the Masks whose voice 88 thought he recognized, but he was not quite sure. They gave him a violent tug and 88 fell to the floor near the fireplace, the embers of which warmed his bare back. They commanded him to kneel with his head and shoulders resting on a low velvet-covered footstool. With his hands tied behind his back, this position proved extremely uncomfortable. He was ordered not to turn around as two of the Masks prised his buttocks apart with their hands and a third penetrated him; he screamed in pain. He was weeping when the rawness of his wound was revived by a fourth Mask who insisted on taking him immediately afterwards, and who then complained that his passage was too tight, that it would have to be widened and tenderized by the serving wenches and, he added with a sneering edge to his voice, also by means of a special method known to the valet Lubomir.

Morella was present throughout and stood by the colonnade taking notes on the corrective treatment which needed to be administered on 88's body. 'Yes, Monsignor,' she answered; 88 realized that there was a man of the cloth amidst the Masks.

The Mask whose voice 88 thought he recognized offered around some malmsey wine, and three of the Masks accepted. He had not yet been whipped, put in a female voice as she stroked his smooth thighs and turned to his lover. Her voice echoed inside the hollow of her Mask as Polissena replied that 88 had only just arrived at Hloboke, that they could however begin just so long as they confined themselves to the legs, the thighs and the fetching tense muscles of his buttocks. At her word, the two serving wenches came in — Morella had probably activated a bell hidden behind the columns. They were followed by Lubomir Zizka who was, as usual, dressed only in his belt, from which dangled the range of whips. Eva and Sona removed them one by one from Lubomir's belt, first the lash, then the riding crop, the whip, the chain and the cat-o'-nine-tails. The dreadful man stood with his groin almost bare — a single whip still hung from his belt. The instruments of torture were laid out on the inlaid table on which there were still some porcelain dishes left over from dinner stained by the juice of ripe mangoes, blackberries and bilberries. Polissena, or rather the Mask which 88 had identified as his lover's, gently approached him and, as she stroked him, she showed him the whips. She caressed them and catalogued each of their particular merits. 'I love you,' she told him.

She picked up a brown riding crop. It was made of tough, sinewy leather; she passed the ends of the firm ropes between his thighs so that he could feel how thick they were. With her gloved hand, she squeezed his testicles with tenderness, not violence. She herself detached the last whip remaining on Lubomir's belt — it was made up of six straps, each of which ended in a knot; she laid it on the table next to the lash of rigid cord and the steel chain which had blurred into the lapis lazuli and the malachite of the inlay.

88 felt fear as he looked at those objects of torture. 'One day they'll give you pleasure. I love you,' repeated Polissena and she kissed him through the veil which fell from her mask. 88 was left standing, looking at the dark lashes, the ropes, the leather whips. It did not even occur to him to refuse even though he had no wish to be whipped. In a voice loaded with persuasive sweetness, Polissena said, 'I want to see you being whipped. Do you accept?'

'I accept,' replied 88.

They decided to kick off with a light cane.

It was useless to cry out, they advised him. No one would hear him: Hloboke nad Vltatov was set in a boundless uninhabited park; his groans would only intensify the excitement of those present. What was more, the first dose of thrashing was only a form of preparation; during his sojourn there, he was going to be flogged regularly. He was not yet docile: he had to subjugate himself and thus belong to Polissena and show her the extent of his love, she explained. By giving himself to her and giving himself to the others, and to the whip, by offering up his striped buttocks to further flogging, he would procure her great pleasure. If he cried out too much, she would have him gagged – but he was free to refuse. 88 did not refuse.

The serving wenches brought him to the colonnade from which hung a chain which 88 had not previously noticed. They hung his bound arms behind his back and attached them to the chain so that they were raised and left his buttocks on display. Lubomir cracked the whip. To begin with, he was lightly beaten with the cane with twenty-second intervals between one beating and the next. 88 did not want to groan or to cry out, he attempted to show strength, to withstand the pain. Then Polissena picked up the small whip and hit him harder on the shins. He moaned uncontrollably.

Polissena handed the whip to a Mask and then to Morella. R.'s bound and proffered body twisted about; the beatings administered by the Mask and then again by Lubomir left him with deep red stripes on his flesh. Lubomir lashed out at his buttocks, trying to centre the rope on the furrow between his thighs.

The five Masks, including his lover, stood around him observing every movement of his body as it writhed about. Then the serving wenches bound his ankles also so that his body was left to wriggle about like an eel. By now he was moaning, and he shouted, 'Enough! That's too much!'

But she enjoyed seeing him twisting about on himself and so he let her go on delighting in his movement. To see him endure those beatings by phalli which soiled and hurt and humiliated him, as well as by whips which racked him with pain, was one way of dominating him. 'That's enough now,' he heard Polissena's voice restraining Lubomir.

'He mustn't learn to like it too much,' 88 heard a female voice urging that he should not get accustomed to the whip.

When they untied him, 88 fell to the floor, his body smeared with blood and sweat, and his face stained with tears.

III

They told him that within the castle – which was run by the Club members, his lover included – there were other numbered men; perhaps he had already glimpsed them in their glass cages. After the initiation period (each one was different from the next), the numbered men were reintegrated into civilian life, but they had to return to the castle at least once a year if it was demanded of them.

Lubomir, 88's valet, was entitled to wake him up during the night and flog him at his pleasure. He was also told that, if Lubomir wanted to gratify himself sexually, he was entitled to that too. Once 88 left the castle, he was secretly to remain at the disposal of any Club member, they told him. His collar and his armbands would betray his education as a man-object: his role as voluntary slave, disposed for anything for the sake of his lover's pleasure.

But it was not much use knowing what his serving wenches or his valet were called as they hardly spoke at all and, were they to have spoken, they would anyway have expressed themselves in a language which 88 could not comprehend. But they all wore their names on a label sewn into their cloaks, just like an American convention or a Japanese package tour. Even the chief serving wench wore her name on her breast so that members could summon her. Morella Pallenberg was allowed to communicate with 88 but only to tell him what he had to do and where he had to go. Communication was impersonally imparted:

Morella's voice had an exotic turn to it, but she was no more identifiable for that.

88 had to spend a lot of time alone in order to be ready for the evenings in which between four and ten Club members took part. Sometimes 88 would be smothered in a hood which did not leave any part of him free except for the triangle for his nostrils and mouth. When he wore the cowl which robbed him of vision, his body would also be similarly covered up. A clinging body-stocking of shiny black elasticated cotton swathed his legs down to the fetters around his ankles, reaching up to his neck, thus covering him completely except for his sex which, with his testicles, was bared in its own black triangle; at the back, his clothing left only the small and mysterious aperture between his buttocks exposed – this would often be violated and widened by different hands, so that the outfit had to be frequently changed. On such occasions, Polissena would protest that 88's face was so handsome that it was a great shame to cover it up; and besides, there was no sport in it if the expressions of fear, surprise, ecstasy or pain in those deeply turquoise eyes which so increased her pleasure were hidden from view.

During the day, 88 would often be taken for a walk in the park. Sometimes Morella Pallenberg led him by the leash. One day Polissena herself had taken him for a walk, flicking a small whip in her other hand; she had untied him to let him run about in the park, then she had reattached his collar.

The park at Hloboke was magnificent. The castle was

surrounded by parkland in the English style which had been planted by the Schwarzenbergs, and was broken up by Italianate gardens with clumps of boxwood hedge interwoven – like in a Primaticcio – with fountains. The hillier parts had been planted in the eighteenth century and looked like a Lancret; the riding school was exquisitely maintained. It looked like something out of Stubbs, with its tall beech hedges upon which the less dexterous Amazons were wont to stumble.

In the leafy grounds one day, in that part of the estate which was landscaped with lakes and small waterfalls and which was known as Sans Souci, they had made him recreate the role of Actaeon; once having untied him, Polissena had disappeared between the branches and 88 had found himself near an Arcadian lake which abounded with flowers – blue and pink lilies splayed out in the water. Given that the park was usually so quiet and deserted, 88 was taken aback to find that, beyond the lilies, he had chanced upon a group of beautiful bathers in those waters. Some of them were swimming about lazily, others lay in the grass, reclining before the ruins of a little Greek temple and caressing one another. Their white and diaphanous skin lying against the watery mosses, and the shadowy depths of the forest confronted him with a spectacle more akin to Boucher than to Titian.

Seeing so much graceful nudity, 88 immediately felt a powerful wave of desire overcome him but, when he saw Polissena as she lay down under the caresses of an excited Callisto, her body jolting delicately as it coiled about in waves of pleasure, he felt himself endangered. Even if he could not see Polissena's face because it was obscured by a golden mask moulded in the classical style, he could recognize her by her soft bosom, her long tapering legs and by her black curls scattered on the grass around her head. But he was lost when his desire — betrayed by his erection — was acknowledged and scoffed at by the nymphs. They started splashing water at him, and to feel his stiffened member; some came up close to him and, from the water, they reached up to lick the impudently uplifted tip of the organ which gave him away. Distracted for an instant from the attentions of her Callisto, Polissena let out an almost savage howl which was then answered by the menacing bays of a pack of dogs at some distance. As the dogs approached the lake, and as 88 was seized by a growing sense of panic (he was still wearing the chain which bound his feet together, and which would render flight both arduous and undignified), he realized that the hounds were nothing other than masked men, other men-objects. They wore canine pelts on their backs and hoods shaped like alsatian muzzles; they barked realistically.

The leading hounds of the pack leapt upon him and set to biting his calves, his buttocks and his back so that 88 was made to understand that the joke would not end there. If Artemis had already turned him into a dog on a leash (even if not exactly into a stag), it was always possible that the men-dogs would tear him to pieces for the delectation of the nymphs and of Polissena. It was his good fortune that human beings possess a weaker sense of smell than dogs, so 88 managed to hide in some azalea bushes and in briar rose, scratching himself all over in the process, and tearing at the wounds inflicted by the whips and the lashes which criss-crossed his skin and gave his body — or at least some parts of it in particular — the look of a grilled steak.

On a different occasion, Polissena had taken him for a walk in the park. From his end of the leash, 88 had dared to ask when he would be free to leave the castle, when his initiation course was to end, whether it was true that, once that first phase at Hloboke nad Vltatov was over, he would have to regard himself as one of the confraternity, and so be ready to offer himself to other members or to present himself on special occasions if she were to order him to do so.

That day she was dressed in nineteenth-century costume, as a horsewoman, with a grey top hat and a veil hanging down over her forehead, a very high collar and a cravat of heavy black silk, a flannel waistcoat in black and white check and a flowing skirt of iron grey wool which reached down to her ankles. She wore nothing underneath.

88 had noticed this when she had mounted the steed and her skirt had gracefully echoed her movement, and ballooned around her.

Another time, when 88 found himself in a small wood along with a group of other numbered men, they were confronted by an awesome vision. A group of ladies, their hair flowing in the wind, their crossbows at the ready, were galloping towards them. One breast was bare and the other was covered by a leather cuirass. But when the arrows began to fly towards them, the terrified men realized that, fortunately, they were not tipped: the heads were actually covered in cotton wool steeped in perfume. They had feared to end up as so many Saint Sebastians.

A kind of complicity was established with the other men-objects (there were a dozen of them in the castle); it was a spirit of frightened conspiracy. Those who had been to Hloboke several times or who had been staying at the castle for at least a month told 88 what to expect. But not one of them discussed the possibility of escape or how to avoid the tricks which were played on them, the floggings which were administered to them, because all of them took pleasure in the state in which they found themselves, that of objects. Quite the contrary, they would sometimes confess that once they left the castle, life became boring for them, that they could no longer re-adapt to normal sexual relations; they preferred their slavish condition, they liked to be treated as things.

They confided that, every now and then, lyrical performances or concerts or Shakespearian tragedies as well as the plays of Racine, Pirandello, Machiavelli and Harold Pinter were put on at Hloboke. 88 had not yet had occasion to take part, but his companions described to him the sublime moments when the sensual weight of the drama and the music burst out in acts which, in the theatre, were only ever inferred. In the last act of *The Marriage of Figaro*, for example, one would see how the protagonists sought to consummate their own frustrated desires. In the final act of *Aida*, after the two had been condemned to death, they ended up naked, in each other's arms in a mortal embrace. As for the Conte di Luna, he would take Leonora right on stage before letting her enter the hideout where she kept Manrico and Azucena imprisoned; and Desdemona was also penetrated on the bastions of Cyprus by her sensual husband. As he invoked the ardent Pleiad, he would tear off his robe and the light blouse from Desdemona's back. Salome of course seduced Narraboth, Herod and Jokanaan which caused a certain amount of annoyance on the part of her mother and of the Tetrarch of Judaea (he did not like the adolescent dedicating her body to others), and the dance of the seven veils was so compelling that the onlookers would become excited and then, in the small theatre of the castle, anything was liable to happen. Naturally, the second act of *Tristan and Isolde* was acted out in protracted copulation between the two protagonists, who would later be caught in flagrante by the king.

Not to speak of the first act of *Der Rosenkavalier* which was performed naked by the Marschallin as Octavian lay in bed; as the music described their reciprocal sexual ecstasy, all that the two singers needed to do was follow the score.

The librettos became more exciting, especially in romantic operas where forbidden acts of passion would be snatched between a moment of inattention on the part of the chorus, and the exit of a husband. In the course of the amorous duet in *Il Ballo in Maschera*, Amelia and the King were almost caught in the act after an extremely speedy coupling and, beneath the veils which Amelia flung upon her person, the plotters not only revealed the wife's identity to her husband, but also bared her naked bosom, still heaving from her recently consumed embrace.

Brünnhilde always wore costumes which kept her breasts bare even if her sexual appetite – especially concerning her nephew Siegfried – was dubious (in that kind of performance, she would more readily couple with Gutrune of whom she was jealous).

The execution of symphonies was also surprisingly explicit and exciting – as in the case of Elgar's Enigma Variations, so the men-objects had assured him.

IV

They also told him of some *déjeuners sur l'herbe* during the course of which a role reversal would take place, and they, the men, would recline naked and available near the women who would be dressed up to the nines, donning straw hats which were overshadowed by poppies and cornflowers, and the food, which was served in wicker baskets set upon coloured trays, would be laid out on cotton napkins upon the grass. Nobody wore a mask during those picnics and the copulations which took place were varied and peculiar. Wearing whips about their belts and goatskin gloves, and conducting conversation of a superior kind (they often discussed business matters in the course of those picnics), it was up to the women to select their mates.

They told him that these enterprising women sometimes made use of mechanical devices, electrically operated
dildoes by means of which they penetrated their men and
each other. 88 had never seen – or even heard of – such
gadgets, so that he was prompted to demand explanations.
He wanted to see them in order to understand what it was
all about. His companions – whether out of good or ill
intent (it would depend upon their own inclinations and
amorous disposition) – told him that these could be found
in all shapes and sizes within that self-same castle. Some
people had their names – or the number of their man –
engraved upon them; there were also plenty of dildoes
bearing the carved images of little eighteenth-century ladies
or of famous views, like that of Prague town hall which, if
gently shaken, produced romantic snowstorms upon the
Hanseatic rooftops and the figures of dainty couples. It was
often the case that the ladies of the castle – as well as the
Club members – were in possession of impressive dildo
collections; some of the examples were famous and indeed
feared for their massive length which was liable to cause
lesions and even fractures.

There were some remote-controlled dildoes which
enabled the owner to possess her object even from a distance. There were blue dildoes and also musical dildoes with
the chimes concealed inside. There were other dildoes
with hidden surprises, like Easter eggs.

His companions had told him that every member of
the Club was given blood tests so that this school of erotic
studies was guaranteed free from Aids. The sexual oasis

therefore enjoyed a very high reputation. It was difficult to become a member – there was a very long waiting list. It boasted no fewer than two hundred members who came from every corner of the earth; they were all under obligation to introduce at least one numbered man every two years. They were sworn to secrecy, as were the men-objects themselves. In any case, who would ever have believed in the existence of a Collegium Feminarum of that sort?

If they were ever recognized outside the four walls of Hloboke, the numbered men could be used by other members, but only if they had the owner's permission. Most of the confraternity – actually a consorority – was made up of famous women: captains of industry, hugely powerful managing directors, stateswomen. A few Czechs had to be included, but they were dangerous and depraved, and they were almost always informers working for the regime.

In the course of one of those evenings, 88 had heard the Baron discussing an important painting. Or rather, 88 was almost sure that the voice was that of Baron von Wurzburg, the one he had met at Bayreuth. And, seeing that he was a well-known collector and that he bought and sold paintings, the conversation was right up his street. The group had not yet moved away from the backless sofa without armrests, upon which Polissena had mounted him and dallied with him in front of some of the members, whilst others – 88 could hear them – were still clustered around the table and went on quaffing delicious wine. Was it absolutely certain, enquired Polissena's voice, that it was a Caravaggio after all? After receiving a brief account,

Polissena was able to understand whence the picture had come: it had been stolen towards the end of the fifties. It came from Palermo, from the Oratorio of S. Lorenzo in the middle of one of the more mafia-riddled quarters of the old city. It had been removed during the night and taken out through the window. The thieves had never been identified; they had been able to carry out their plan without disturbance.

It was one of the better-known canvases by Caravaggio. Such an important work, a work which was so notoriously stolen, could never appear in the auction houses or in private or public collections. This work was now in Prague, they told her; Marian had it in safekeeping and the Monsignor was involved in the affair.

It was not so odd that the picture should have ended up in Czechoslovakia, said Polissena; that kind of thief, once having been seized by panic and having realized that the work was not saleable, usually came to an agreement with some insurance company or with the state; alternatively, he would destroy it, or else he would turn to one of the countries which do not uphold international law. It had probably been imported in secret and sold to the Czech government in exchange for something else. In any case, there was no one but the Czechs to buy it. Given that Sicily was the land of mafia and Czechoslovakia the land of machine-guns, it was clear to her, so Polissena concluded, in what the trade-off consisted.

The Baron pursued the topic; he proposed that she should bring back the canvas to the West in her baggage;

as the director of a famous institution, Polissena was effectively covered if the canvas were to be found in her personal suitcase. Anyway, she would be given an official letter from the Ministry attributing the painting to a Flemish master and authorizing its export. The letter would be written by Marian and the declaration was to be backed up by the Narodni Galerie Praha. A third female voice – unfamiliar to 88 – suggested that the canvas be cut up into four or five parts, just as they did in the nineteen-hundreds so as to render it unrecognizable. A few extra details might be added in, and then it could be sold in different markets at different times. Caravaggio's hand was incontrovertible and clearly recognizable so expert opinion would be genuine, the profits to be made were enormous and Polissena could then buy the small head of the Madonna for the Louvre, so lending credibility to the discovery and crowning herself with prestige. The other segments would not be sold publicly, said a third voice, so as not to arouse any suspicion. Polissena went on insisting that she wanted to have nothing to do with a stolen Caravaggio, that the game was not worth the candle.

88 detested the Baron because he suspected that he was the one who had raped him and penetrated him with his hands and asked that they keep him open at night using special springs which widened his passage. Or maybe it was Marian who had violated him, and the Baron was the one who had had himself penetrated after 88 had been aroused by female hands and artful lips. Sometimes, from within the obscurity of his mask and smothered by the

deafening sounds of ascetic and aggressive compositions by Britten or Benjamin, he had no idea who was taking him; was it Polissena who proffered her mouth and who then guided his swollen penis into her womb? Or was it some other woman?

During one of these evenings, maybe it was the fourth or the fifth that he spent at Hloboke, they had blindfolded him and then made him kneel down. A gloved hand – could it have been Polissena's? – caressed him, and her voice had then ordered him to carry on on his own. He did not want to, nor did he like to; it embarrassed him and he feared that he would be unable to but, as soon as he put up a protest, they called Morella and Lubomir to whip him. At that point, 88 took up his labours once more. Wearing his mask, he felt less ashamed to carry out that almost mechanical act, paraded in front of the other members; it was not aesthetic and it certainly was not very private. Then they pushed him and he felt himself falling, his chest coming to rest on one of the petit-point cushions. Perhaps somebody was about to penetrate him. He hated those violent penetrations which lacerated his body. But he would not have complained or protested. He let himself go on the cushion when he realized that whoever it was had changed his mind. They then had him lifted off the cushion and he found himself kneeling with his chest supported: a pair of legs had wound themselves around his neck and were squeezing him. 88 understood that his mouth would not be spared.

He could not always understand whom he was penetrating; if, at certain moments, he had recognized Polissena by her touch, her gasps, her vigorous contortions, he had then been overcome by doubt and even by the certainty that, after they had delighted in each other, she had been substituted by another woman.

Returning to his cell, 88 reflected on how bizarre it was not to recognize the body he had had.

V

His cell looked like one of the rooms he had walked through on his first day; it was laid out with wide steps covered in very thick carpeting which doubled up as a mattress. 88 would lie on one or other of the steps whilst Lubomir would sometimes snore further down and even Morella was wont to spend some hours of the night with them. On the walls were various hooks to which chains could be attached and which would then be linked into his collar, his armbands and the fetters around his ankles. He always slept naked and bound, but he had never considered escaping; the idea had not even crossed his mind.

Sometimes, in the middle of the night, he would suddenly be woken up and flogged by his valet who always administered the beatings as if he were quite furious. Lubomir was horrible. His hair was sparse and curly, his neck virtually non-existent, he had a porcine face, sweated profusely, smelt bad and filled the cell with his foetid emanations, grunting noisily in his sleep throughout the night.

Lubomir would gaze at 88 for ages as he slept before

raping or flogging him. He admired the beauty of his athletic body, of his classical head, of those curly locks around his small ears: he would stare at the long lashes resting on his taut young skin. Sometimes Lubomir would chain 88 up by the ankles, the arms and the neck; then he would whip him. 88 screamed with pain inside that cell, especially when the lash found a groove where he had already been beaten. Then Lubomir, armed with his tumescent, heavy sex and invigorated by the wriggling movements of 88's body, would mount him from behind and, keeping him trussed up, he would spray the abundance of his enormous phallus into 88's body.

Lubomir used on occasion to hang him up with his hands tied behind his back and a brass chain pulling him up towards the ceiling, and his ankles also bound. The sight of that handsome body arching beneath the blows of the whip as if caught in a spasm of desire would once more swell the throbbing organ of the ghastly valet.

The other numbered men had confessed to him more than once that they too hated their personal valets. Sometimes the same valet would be assigned to two men at once. 88 should consider himself lucky as some valets were much more disgusting and malodorous than Lubomir. There were dwarfs, as well as horrid Japanese with extravagantly sagging buttocks who could only ever be satisfied by the lips of their victims. The Japanese always wanted the mouths of their numbered men to be glossy with scarlet lipstick. Into these painted targets they would insert their phalli. Often they demanded that the object-men make themselves up with cosmetics or otherwise it was up to the serving wenches to dust them with scented powders and blushers. Their buttocks had to be pleasingly pink and their tighter, more secret lips had also to be painted. If the numbered men did not behave as they were told to and did not stimulate those awful pyramids of flesh, the foetid and deformed valets would thrash them mercilessly.

88 bore the mark of the whip all over his body; some deeper stripes crossed other violet-coloured ones. As soon as they healed, new blows would be inflicted on his person.

But one thing was certain: 88 did not entertain the notion of escape. Maybe he would not have been able to escape from his cell or from the inside of the castle but, when he was out for a walk in the park, he could at least have thought about it. Instead, all he yearned for was the return of his lover. He longed for a normal embrace, for the kind of passion which had first and immediately drawn them together without any false inhibitions. He wanted to go back to lying beside her body, to talk to her and listen to the sound of her voice, to enjoy her. She was full of fascination, even in the way she moved. She had a melodious voice. She would ask for things, even when her requests were really commands. 88 had noticed how often men and women alike fell prey to her fascination, to her dark but piercing looks. Her big eyes with their pearly wet corneas gave her a look of fragility like a frightened *schvec*. But Polissena certainly was not fragile.

Even those first chapters in their past which had initially stunned him (like their first encounter in the

103

prisons of Monpleasance, or their unbridled copulation in the car behind Louis' back), now, as he remembered them, they struck him as almost tame, as memories to which to devote nostalgic thoughts.

But he did not feel forsaken by her. Far from it. Polissena was often present at the evening entertainments which punctually took place in the dining room-cum-library with its old leather and superbly inlaid table.

Morella divulged that it was Polissena who ordered his extra-fine meals, who thought up those games and chose his serving wenches.

It could have been evening number seven. After making every conceivable use of his body, the Club members had returned to eating around the table which had, on that occasion, been laid with particular care and extreme luxury.

The dining table at Hloboke nad Vltatov was always breathtaking; it was covered with tablecloths of magnificent lace, with lustrous seventeenth-century silver, and porcelain and crystal and even amber candelabra. The cutlery was copious and flanked Meissen plates, and numerous goblets which were exquisitely crafted and tinkled with the finest wines. The courses were served in enchanting and imaginative combinations.

That evening, whilst the guests – they numbered six or seven (no more than ten participants were ever allowed) – had sat themselves down again around the table and had returned to sipping ruby-coloured port and consuming soft cheeses served in cow- and goat- and sheep-shaped moulds, according to the type of milk from which they had been fermented, 88 had remained on the floor watching them.

They had helped themselves from a dish made of mother-of-pearl which had been brought to the table by an extravagantly dressed valet whose tail trailed between his buttocks.

The company helped themselves to lightly cooked oysters which dripped with cream and saffron, and to baby clams which tickled with ginger and cinnamon. They sipped Alsatian wines from magnificent goblets of Bohemian manufacture, of course.

The valet arrived with each course, but they were actually served by maids dressed – or rather, undressed – just like maids of the thirties, those that featured in Deanna Durbin or Cary Grant films with starched aprons and highly stylized bibs. The aprons of these graceful maids only covered part of their bellies, so that their movements and the shadow of their mons veneris could be glimpsed. Their breasts were also free from the starched lace fabric which reached up to their diaphragm. Each one led a numbered man who was tied to the end of a chain. In their turn, these carried silver trays and, as the guests consumed their shellfish, the trays piled up with discarded shells. Too close to the naked round buttocks supported on vertiginously high heels and therefore capriciously tilted, the numbered men could not be insensible to such nudity as they stood silently behind them.

Now and then, unable to resist, an object would take possession of a maid, or else a guest would rise from the table and have herself penetrated by the men-objects. The others watched, though not all of them did; often they just went on eating their delicious foods. It was on that very evening that the enormous silver dish-cover was raised from a large tray carried by four maids and four numbered men, revealing a marvellous male body almost hidden beneath the seaweed, the sauces and the shellfish. The guests had flung themselves upon him, eating the seafood which he bore on his stomach, tearing the langoustines from his armpits, the caviar from his mouth, licking at it with the tips of their tongues around his groin, amongst his hairs, picking at the little clusters lodged in his belly button. The edible man shivered and shuddered with pleasure. Then they threw him into the swimming pool.

But before the forcible immersion, the masked revellers had returned to that subject which had intrigued 88 a couple of days previously: they were talking about the Caravaggio painting. The canvas had already been cut up and carefully divided, someone was saying; all that was needed now was for someone to take it out of Czechoslovakia. They needed to begin by selling one of the sections in order to test the market. The *Rude Prado* had publicized the news that an unknown Caravaggio had turned up in Switzerland; the picture, they had said, was probably a study for the canvas removed thirty years previously from the Oratorio di S. Lorenzo in Palermo. It shared various similarities in the materials used and the figures depicted. The article voiced no doubts as to the authenticity of the painting, related the director of the Narodni Galerie.

This article, insisted the voice, suggested that the canvas was virgin and indicated the provenance in this way in order to facilitate its sale. He added that Milos Cechok, the deputy director of the Brno museum, who specialized in the late Italian Renaissance, was writing a scholarly text on Caravaggio and on the rediscovery of the canvas which had been taken from Switzerland to Czechoslovakia. Showing a certain amount of imagination, he was retracing a moment in the later life of the painter during which Caravaggio supposedly painted a group of small canvases, one of which had indeed been found in Switzerland.

He was to receive 0.15 per cent of the commission for his contribution, continued the voice, and all the more so because Professor Cechok was an inexhaustible fund of unexceptionable scholarly tracts. There was, for instance, that small Cimabue stolen from Poggibonsi forty-odd years ago which was just waiting to be rediscovered.

The sale of the five sections of the Caravaggio amounted to a huge transaction, continued the voice. He had spoken of it with the Monsignor who was expert in such matters. He suggested that Dauphine or Valentina, one of Polissena's secretaries, should carry a couple of the segments out of Czechoslovakia as soon as possible. He said that Sotheby's as well as Christie's were agog with the rumours going about concerning the lost Caravaggio. The whole thing should be built up with television documentaries and films about the young Caravaggio; there was certainly no shortage of homosexual directors to make such films.

In view of the prices attained by Impressionists, post-

Impressionists, Van Gogh and so on, was it not advisable to work with those and leave the Renaissance alone? queried Polissena's voice. She was still bent on keeping out of the deal. Van Goghs were difficult to steal and dismember, came the reply. How would you set about cutting up a canvas of sunflowers, for instance? Or landscapes of Arles? Or views of Provence vineyards? Polissena said she was much happier with the idea of dismembering a Van Gogh, instead of a Caravaggio. And she would have been quite content at the prospect of cutting up a Renoir into six, seven, even into sixty-seven fragments.

VI

On the following day 88 heard Polissena insisting that the others should not penetrate him from the rear; 88 would be leaving the castle within a few hours and she did not want him to be unfit for travel. Somebody asked her if she would yield him: surrendering an object was not an inconceivable demand between intimate friends and fellow Club members. What if he lost Polissena, or was abandoned by her? But she instead replied that she could not even take the suggestion into consideration as 88 was hers and hers alone for the moment.

If one day she had asked 88 to give himself out of love for her, he would certainly have obliged – otherwise the course at the Castle would prove to have been ineffectual. But she, Polissena, desired him to be by her side. 88 still had a lot to learn from her, from the castle, from himself. He did not yet realize what his body and his mind were capable of doing – they were going to explore those avenues together.

Some hours later, Morella refitted his chastity belt, then the serving wenches arrived with a buzz saw and severed the fetters around his ankles (but they left his armbands and the collar intact), and they told him that it was time for him to go.

It came as a shock that his apprenticeship was at an end: the revelation was almost brutal. He was not expecting it and he felt lost. In fact, he had not believed Polissena's words; he had become accustomed to the new routine.

He was frightened of walking through the great entrance hall which he had not seen since that first day when Polissena had dropped him off on the broad sweep of gravel in front of the castle; he was scared of finding himself in front of the main door of Hloboke, of crossing the threshold, of finding himself alone. Would Polissena be waiting for him?

The door which he had passed through on the first day of his initiation had remained a mystery because, whenever they had taken him for walks in the park at the end of his leash, he had gone out by the east wing, or else by the great southern entrance of the castle. He walked past the great staircase, through the room dominated by the portrait of Eleonora Schwarzenberg in the midst of Flemish tapestries, and on an ebony table he found an album which he signed, '88, object'.

First he had to go to the neo-gothic chapel of Hloboke

where his number was to be blessed by Monsignor Ermenegildo Venini, Argentinian legate to the Holy See and another member of the Club. It had become traditional, explained Morella, for every new object to be sanctified. In addition, he was obliged to pledge himself to secrecy, obedience and loyalty to the confraternity. In Latin, of course. The function droned on and 88 could hardly wait to clasp Polissena in his arms once more. But would she be there? He caught a glimpse of Monsignor Ermenegildo Venini by the altar, his back turned towards the congregation, in the old-fashioned manner of celebration. He fingered the chalice and the precious objects with his long hands: it clearly gave him great pleasure.

Wearing the same clothes as he had worn on that first day, his bright blue eyes blinded by the light which shone through the summer rain, 88 finally pushed the huge handles of antique wood and walked outside. There she was! She was seated in the car, waiting for him. She hugged him as if they had not seen each other in all that time, as if the masked Polissena present at those evening parties at the castle was not the self-same person. She stroked his hair and savoured his ears, rediscovering his small nose with the tip of her tongue.

'Where are we going?' he asked her.

They could talk to one another at last: he could ask her questions!

'Malastrana,' she replied, with a smile revealing her shiny teeth, and her eyes filled with promise.

PART THREE

I

They spoke little as the rain dripped down on the tarmac outside, on the ochre-coloured sheaves of corn and the leafy tree-tops. The windows of the car were striped with rain and misted up on the inside.

Now and then Polissena touched his face and kissed him on the ears. 'I love you,' she would say to him.

R. was driving the car and had found his suitcase in the boot in exactly the same position in which he had left it. And on the back seat lay his bag with the now outdated newspapers, his business diary, his calling cards.

Leaning on the backrest, he could feel the laceration of those wounds, those blows which had striped his back, his buttocks, his thighs. Some of the lashings had left deep, purple marks. Others had disappeared from one day to the next.

She kept her legs apart on the leather which stuck to the skin of her naked thighs. 'I don't like Czechs,' she informed him. They were still in the České Budějovice region.

She did not like Germans, nor did she like Czechs, yet she took him to Germany and Czechoslovakia. 'We won't stay much longer,' she went on. 'A couple of days, that's all, so you get to see Prague: it's a magnificent city.'

'Is there much to see?' His blue eyes left the road for a moment and gazed at her.

'Loads; it's a shame they're so slimy.'

'What do you mean?'

'You'll see.' She kissed him on the belly button which she tracked down by undoing a button of his shirt. Through the fabric, he could feel the chastity belt and above that the armbands and the collar around his neck. How much would he be subjugated? How much could she ask of him? How far could R.'s docility stretch? She could feel the grooves which the whip had left on his soft skin.

'You're not free,' she notified him.

'I know,' R. replied.

'Do you accept?'

'Yes, I accept.'

'Are you angry with me?'

'No.'

'I love you,' she repeated; 'I delight in you, I rejoice in you through all the things you let me do to you and with you.' Her black curls were heaped on her forehead, her lips were tight and heart-shaped, painted a brilliant red which went well with her blouse and the silk rose pinned to her bosom.

R. knew he was hers and wanted it thus, that much he had by now decided. The belt which strapped in his groin bore continual testimony to this, reminding him that he belonged to her, that he owed her whatever his lover demanded of him. Offering up his body to her, his sex exposed, his mouth gaping as he groaned, was part of being subjected to her. His function was to make her enjoy his acceptance.

'I love you,' she told him again with a sigh.

It was what he wanted to know.

So long as it was true. How could she love him as she said she did if she then subjected him to torture and surrendered him to others? Giving him away was a means of proving to herself that R. belonged to her, but it was also a means of depriving him of any individuality.

How would she have reacted if R. had been different? Often R. was not even sure that he had possessed her rather than some other woman in that castle, in the course of those evenings. He was almost ashamed of having entered another body without being absolutely sure whose body it was. But why wasn't Polissena jealous when others made use of his body?

The roads they were driving down were asphalted but narrow; they seemed unused to either traffic or tourists. They lacked the infrastructure characteristic of the West, the petrol stations and road markings. The landscape was hilly and green. They stopped at Tabor, the capital of Jan Huss, the heretical Bohemian theologian. In the ancient town hall with its spiky vaults was an exhibition dedicated to the Hussite Movement. It consisted of photocopies and maps, ragged scraps of material, bits of bone and metal and the odd stone. 'A didactic and virtually non-existent exhibition typical of dictatorial regimes,' she said sententiously; 'they're meant for schoolchildren and the proletariat, so that they of course grow up hating museums and these kinds of exhibitions.'

She was irritated by the amount of time they had made her waste, and by the tickets which they had been induced to buy in order to view a few rags.

Tabor clung to a steep hillside. It was gothic with a touch of Renaissance and baroque also; the façades of the buildings were ornate and the colours rich – sienna, amaranthine, burnt sienna, pale cobalt. The square was wide, like all the squares of those Hanseatic townships; it was festooned with baroque saints; painted clocks adorned the pointed towers, saints and Virgin Marys surrounded by marble clouds and mawkish angels surmounted the fountains. 'Shall we have something to drink?' asked Polissena, heading straight for the bar on the corner which was tucked under a crooked house weighed down by its antiquity. The bar was sad but homely and not without charm. Its windows were all polished and the few bottles which were displayed on the shelves were reflected in the Art Deco rhomboids.

They served tea and coffee as well as slivovitz and wine.

'*Dobre jitro.*'

Polissena took R. by surprise when she answered, '*Nemluvin cesky . . . prosin.*' She looked around and added, '*Lamev vina.*'

A bottle of light and slightly acidic white wine arrived shortly thereafter. From the label, they discovered that the wine was Moravian but Polissena commented that these days the Czechs were not even able to make their own wine, so they bought it wholesale from Hungary and stuck bogus local labels on it.

R. sipped it with pleasure, looking at Polissena through his parted lashes over those blue eyes which she liked so much. Prague was about eighty kilometres away.

'We're going to stay with Marian, a friend. Do you remember him?' she asked.

R. knew that not only had he been a visitor at Hloboke, but also that it was probably he who had ravished him at Bayreuth. He remembered him vaguely: off-putting moustache over lips which were excessively rosy for a man.

'He has a lovely apartment in the old city.'

'Why don't we go to a hotel instead?' suggested R. He was not keen to stay with Marian, and he wanted to be left alone with his lover.

'That would be rude and besides, he works in the museum. I have to go back there to see their reserve collection; there are paintings there which I've never seen. In any case, Prague hotels are always full unless you slip the doorman a few dollars. You've always got to tip around here – in dollars. It's so tiresome, and I'm not even very good at it.'

'It takes a special knack to slip a forbidden bank note into someone's hands. I'm no good at it either.'

Talking to each other and touching one another every now and then, catching one another's eye and smiling at each other, they reached Prague before midday.

He drove without concentrating; there was not much

traffic. Every now and then, R.'s thoughts turned on Monpleasance, on the immense distance separating him from his kin – a cultural distance, an inconceivable distance. No one there knew where he was – not that his mother had ever shown any interest in the movements of her children, or any anxiety, for that matter; but, at this point, he might as well get in touch with her and tell her where he was. Should he send her a postcard? Signed by Polissena, Cousin Polissena? He savoured the notion that they would come to know that he and Polissena . . . nothing else, that much was certain. His father would glance at the postcard with indifference: Czechoslovakia? Where was it? Geography had never been his forte, he had never enjoyed travelling and, anyway, he did not know a single language apart from a tight-lipped English.

But maybe now that R. was nearing his twenty-seventh birthday, they would wonder where in the world their youngest son had ended up. Not that they had ever remembered his birthday; the odd present had reached him, usually a couple of weeks after the fateful day, together with excuses. 'We were so busy, dear . . .' and yet his father and mother had nothing to do apart from fox-hunting.

Suddenly they were nearing Prague. The roads – in conformity with the unwritten code of all dictatorial regimes – were transformed as they neared the capital: now it was all roaring motorways, huge thoroughfares lined by signposts bearing the letters 'Praha'. Even under the rain, in that greenish light, Prague appeared unreal and incredibly beautiful.

They had emerged on to the river Moldava which forked around an emerald island quivering with rain, gardens and white swans. The city unveiled itself before R.'s eyes: the golden pinnacles, the leaden domes; the colours seemed to dart about and pile up on one another in a turbulent jumble of centuries and shades and producing an exhilarating effect.

Polissena – who seemed to know the city quite well, heaven only knew how – tossed her black curls with her hand and complemented the spectacle with a running commentary bursting with enthusiasm. 'Down there – d'you see? – is the opera house. Ahead, there's Hradcany, the castle. Right up at the top, yes. There's the museum.'

Now and then she smoothed some greasy dark lipstick on her mouth as if wanting to appear especially seductive. It was clear that she was happy to be able to show such a beautiful city to her lover. There was something maternal and protective about her attitude. You could not cross the old bridge which sprouted with statues, she explained; it was for pedestrians only, but they would wander over it later, they would contemplate it once more, they would go for endless walks on the following day. It was in any case the shortest route to the old city of Malastrana.

'The statues . . . the baroque . . . the colours . . .' she sounded almost like a tourist guide except that she would always conclude, 'it's a pity they're so awful.'

The Malastrana district – small city (though the name suggested something much more sinister in any Latin language) – was spread out under the castle. It was the newest part of the old city, as it were, given that it was built in the eighteenth century and had remained just the same, frozen in time: the architraves, the leather-bound doors of the taverns and churches, the little lanes, the fine staircases. The enamel shop-signs were still there, as were the vaults over the arcades running along the streets, meshing into and crossing over one another in the corners of the squares. The chiming of the bells was still the same, and the narrow steps and the great gates of gilded wrought iron. Even the gardens carved out of the rock of the mountain and dug into the sandy shores of the river were lush with boxwood and set out with white wistaria between the gravel paths in accordance with eighteenth-century good taste.

They went through Letenska and entered into Malostranske Nam where they parked the car with some difficulty between the tangle of interlocking tramlines embedded in the tarmac which crossed over one another in a network known only to the metal hulks which tripped along the maze, sure of themselves as they tinkled and lurched with their loads of gossiping students. They climbed up a street which narrowed into steps, and passed before wiggly stuccoed façades painted in pink and gold, in apple green and dusty blue.

'Isn't she beautiful?' Polissena went on asking as if she were referring to a person. 'A shame that she's full of Czechs!' For her, it was like saying, 'Shame that your breath stinks.' Or, 'Pity you've a wart on your nose.'

In through the small door lacquered in dark blue gloss, up the stairs, on the third floor.

Marian had bought the apartment with the money of an American antiques dealer with whom he did business that was certainly illegal. So he said that half of it belonged to his friend, though his friend never came as he could never obtain an entry visa. Polissena suspected that Marian had a hand in prejudicing those visits.

Young, a small moustache protruding over his fleshy lips, you only had to look at him to know that he was not to be trusted. Even R. who was an innocent, a Prince Mishkin figure, did not let himself be carried away by his characteristic charity towards others; he decided that Marian must be a spy for the regime.

He was perfectly correct.

He greeted them with quiet enthusiasm. He slurred his words as if letting them plop out with his saliva so that they became unpleasant, and you tended to listen to the sound rather than to grasp the content. Marian's apartment consisted of four rooms: a library-cum-studio, two bedrooms and a kitchen-cum-dining room. There was quite a large bathroom, but only one. Every window gave on to some golden spire, on to ochre and grey piazzas.

Marian despatched a boy to fetch the luggage from the car 'before it's stolen', he specified. 'Do you have any money?' he asked R. who never did have any, but who pulled out of his pocket a couple of bank notes.

'No, not koronas. Real money, dollars. You can't buy anything here with koronas. Even English pounds are better than local currency.' He had changed all the pounds he had, confessed R. Marian silently registered him as incompetent and idiotic. Polissena thrust forward a green piece of paper. 'You buy everything in dollars,' she whispered to R. 'It's forbidden but that's why they like it. Never do anything here according to the rules: they have no taste for it. Hotels, restaurants, bodies and souls: everything is transacted in dollars.'

The two beds in their bedroom were separated by a shamelessly Liberty chest; a painted angel supported the walnut table; in its turn, the winged human form disappeared in folds of drapery and flights of wings and foam of painted porcelain. The corner shelf was embellished in the same style, though lighter, with extravagant cascades of overlay: a sort of Slavic Lalique. The library was of course stuffed with books which were almost all forbidden on both political and moral grounds, and the mere fact that they were so conspicuously exposed made it evident that Marian was allowed to behave exactly – or very nearly – as he wanted. On the backs of the books were imprinted the prohibited names of Kafka, de Sade, Nietzsche and Rimbaud. There was *Les Fleurs du Mal*, and a whole lot of Kleist, Büchner and Wedekind. A load of magnificently diseased literature.

The space which was not taken up by books was instead covered by prints of Old Prague with a few sinister or bizarre characters promenading around the old ghetto or near the Old-New Synagogue perhaps. The Golem in these dark engravings overpowered terrified damsels; the odd phantom struggled in the wells on Hradcany; a sarcophagus seen from the inside depicting a desperate figure (clearly buried by mistake) adorned those walls in an excess of morbidity.

The lithographs and detailed engravings shared something in common with Odilon Redon, though the content was manifestly Kafkaesque.

'People die on these streets,' murmured Marian who had been observing R.'s fascinated gaze lingering in amazement on the fragile, grey imprinted ghosts of Prague.

'What?' R. found Marian unusual and unpleasant.

He turned himself around as somebody had just entered the room. It was not Polissena who had stayed in their bedroom to make herself up: it was a girl with big blue eyes and black eyelashes, fine lips and pale skin. 'Marina Kosiche,' announced Marian without bothering to introduce him to her. Maybe he had forgotten his name. 'She works at the Cedok: she might prove useful to you.'

He was right to be proud of her: Marina was splendid, perfect, all new, with wavy black hair and white hands. She looked like Hedy Lamarr. She carried a package under her arms. 'It's the Caravaggio,' Marian confided in R. But R. thought he should know nothing of that painting, given that no one had officially told him anything about it. He had overheard verbal exchanges regarding the 'Nativity' with S. Laurence and S. Francis when he had been an object in the castle; he should not then have listened. He looked at Marian without uttering a word.

Polissena came in; her lipstick was so dark and shiny that her mouth looked as if it had been painted black. They were like orchids, those palpitating lips. Her eyelids were shaded in bright blue. She shook Marian's hand as she looked at it with suspicion, and suggested to R. that they

121

should go out at once: they would wander about Prague before dining all together.

'Prague has lost that cobweb colour which it had for centuries,' Marian informed them. 'But you shouldn't take any notice of the new colours which dress her up: her soul is still putrid.'

'They use low quality paints,' added Marina. It was the first time that she had spoken and she uttered the words with a small, childish, melodious voice. 'So they peel off straight away. Goldleaf has been replaced by purple, and strawberry red has been substituted for the old crimson.'

Funny that someone from the Cedok should talk thus, thought Polissena — she was over-educated too.

'I've got the Caravaggio,' broke in Marian.

'Which one?' asked Polissena in surprise.

'Here. In a package.' And he pointed at the object wrapped in brown paper and fastened with transparent string which Marina had laid on the table near the windows which were shaded by dirty white lace curtains.

The windows which were decorated in this fashion led on to a balcony. From the package, Marian pulled out a board swathed in cotton wool and felt. It was about 60 cm by 45 cm. It depicted a squatting Madonna illuminated from below; the child lay down near her skirt on a straw bed barely covered in white cloth which caught the light side on. Next to her, on her left, a young shepherd with blond hair was turned towards the heavens. Polissena knew that, up there, the two saints upon whom the young and finely featured shepherd fixed his gaze were St Francis and St James who were now cut out of the picture. The enchantment of the sad face of this very young Madonna, her pallor, her right hand chastely shielding her bosom, moved Polissena deeply. How could one not be moved before that masterpiece which had gone missing for so many years?

'Look, Marian, I don't want to have anything to do with it. Stolen paintings are too hot for me. Believe me, it's not just a question of my not being able to handle it: I don't want to either. And you too, I must say, you who work for a museum, shouldn't touch it. These things always come out into the open.'

'But it's unrecognizable.'

That was not the case. The composition of the Madonna, the child and the shepherd had been carved up in such a way as not to provoke any suspicions as to the havoc played upon the patina of the paint and the grain of the canvas by the scissors. It was touched up with brush-strokes which would probably show up under X-ray but which conferred upon the canvas the integral look of a finished image. It might convince some.

'Special paints were used which age under heat,' explained Marian. 'There's no analysis that can show up the new patches, the tears or the cuts. We're safe as houses.'

'And how many did you get out of it?'

'There are four sections of different sizes: St Lawrence is long and tall, very elegant, a kind of Zurbarán. They'll have some trouble acknowledging it as a Caravaggio. The angel with the Gloria in Excelsis Deo had to suffer a little for the sake of the head of St Lawrence and the ass. Then there's St Francis with the other saint, which is the smallest of all – you have it before you: a marvel.'

'In any case, Marian, I don't like to see a Caravaggio hacked to pieces and I have every intention of staying on as director of the Louvre. That's all I have to say on the matter. Now let's go and see the ghetto.' And she took R. by the hand, trailing him behind her like a child, an object.

Having arrived in Czechoslovakia back in 1938, the Nazis – assisted by the local population – had had all the time and opportunity to gas the entire Jewish population. So that in the Prague ghetto – famous throughout history – there was not a single Jew left. Or perhaps there were just a couple. They were rarer than a Caravaggio. Marian had also voiced his opinion on the subject. 'They asked for it: they made common cause with the Sudeten Germans, never with us. It was always with them, with the Germans, that they did business. My father told me the same. And my grandfather before him: the Jews never mixed with the Czechs, so we didn't help them.'

They had not mixed with the Czechs when they were shut up inside the walls of the ghetto and forced to live in cramped little spaces.

Those walls had crumbled in the first years of the century, not out of liberal zeal but as a result of real estate speculation. All that was left were five synagogues. The Germans had blown up all the others. But these, the oldest of which was a complex structure of wood and stone dating back to 1270, had been turned into museums. The Nazis themselves had planned the museum as a place in which to exhibit the collected works of a vanished race, so they planned to call it.

In the synagogues, which hummed with tourists, were objects of Hebrew worship, objects of great value which came from despoiled synagogues, from looted houses, from massacred people and families crammed into airless trains; the Nazis had wanted to keep those works of artistic merit in order to conserve the cultural heritage of the race which they had planned to wipe off the face of the earth. There was something supremely bourgeois and genteel about the idea; their intention could even be considered – blasphemously – as lacking a sense of humour. To plan to kill all and yet at the same time to maintain a cultural testimony: what perversion!

Now the Cedok had taken it in hand and their coaches arrived unloading hundreds of tourists who paid their entrance fee and snapped their photographs. Filing into the Old-New Synagogue, they would glance at the Taled and the sacred cloths, the objects of veneration, the sixteenth-century embroidery, and then they would launch themselves into the cemetery, clambering over the tombs, clicking their cameras all the while, without even looking around them: they would view the processed images once they got home. For the moment, there was no time: they had to take more photographs.

For the price of a double ticket, you could go to the synagogue where the pictures of children incinerated at Mathausen were displayed. In a fourth synagogue – after paying another supplement – you could look at more photographs, letters and testimonials of those who had been tortured and butchered.

In order to gain entrance to the Jewish cemetery, you had to buy yet another ticket. The tombs had jostled against one another for centuries: there had never been enough room. It looked like a mouth full of crooked teeth made of antique ivory; the headstones bore inscriptions in Hebrew – dates, together with the names of the great rabbis – these restricted the trees which consequently squeezed through between the stelae, their roots sucking up nourishment several metres down. Beneath the stones was layer upon layer of bodies and monuments, as well as more funerary stones. Shortage of space had always confined both the quick and the dead, all squashed together within the Prague ghetto.

II

Ghosts seemed to wander about the other streets as well. In the Café Jugenstil near Wenceslas Square, R. and Polissena ate a duck – subject to slipping a bank note into the straining hand of the head-waiter.

'What did Marian mean when he said that people die on the streets of Prague?' asked R. looking about him with flickering blue eyes. All he could see were tourists and his own image reflected and bounced off in multiple images.

And it was raining. 'They die of cold, that's for sure.'

'Marian is as sinister as Prague herself,' replied Polissena, a gold-coloured lipstick in her hand, and then on her lips. She traced the movement from memory, without looking in the mirror, in the mirrors.

'Why are we staying with him then?'

'We're colleagues, maybe there's no real reason. Next week he's off to Rome where he's got business as well as friends, or so he tells me. He wants me to meet Monsignor Venini, Ermenegildo Venini. He's the Argentinian Legate at the Holy See and Marian wants me to look at some paintings. It's a bit fishy; if Marian were just an academic, he wouldn't of course be able to come and go from Czechoslovakia as he does, or to Paris or Rome, for that matter.'

'What's his business in Rome?'

'Paintings.'

'And what's all this about a Caravaggio?' R.'s long lashes shaded his eyes. Polissena wondered whether he was really interested, or whether in any case it suited her to explain it all to R. What could he understand about Michelangelo Merisi? How could he comprehend the beauty and the purity of those hands, of those silks bathed in celestial light?

'It's some fraud or other,' was all she told him; 'don't lose any sleep over it.' They stopped in taverns stacked with barrels of rich-smelling wood, with golden shop-signs, and doors padded with leather, furnished with walnut tables. Out of the blurry eyes of the drunks, the melancholics and the desperate issued the phantasms of thought,

127

the shadows of sadness. Out came the strains of Janáček together with all those other dark sentiments of Czechoslovakia.

Later they dined in one of those famous Malastrana restaurants in the elegantly finished room at the back, procured by means of dollars, in which the fire flickered in the hearth and there were only five tables, laid with discernment: the linen starched and splendid, the wine served in gleaming goblets and the crockery made of fine porcelain.

As with all those economies gone mad, there were no fresh vegetables – or very nearly none – to be found in Czechoslovakia, even in high summer.

Afterwards, Polissena settled the bill in dollars: the others had not even made half-hearted attempts to do the honours for her, or to snatch away the weighty bill.

The others consisted of Marian, Marina and Vladislav Huk, head of the Bratislava opera, the one with white hair whom R. had already met at Bayreuth.

Valentina Bulova had also turned up. She was one of Polissena's secretaries: R. remembered her all too well. She was slightly altered in that she had had her hair cut and streaked in magenta. Her black eyes and fleshy lips were evenly arranged on her small face framed by thick hair which, though now cropped, formed a kind of pointed crest, inadvertently punk. Valentina dressed very smartly: she wore a well-cut jacket around her tapered waist and a tailored skirt over her rounded calves.

'Did you know that the woman who bought the Van

Gogh,' Valentina was saying, 'the one who comes from California, has a wax finger attached to her stump with an emerald ring? But, unlike her finger, the emerald is genuine.'

'But she isn't,' commented Polissena; 'her wax finger is the only original thing about her.'

'Don't tell me that you don't like her Van Goghs,' said Marian, sounding slightly scandalized.

'He's hateful ever since he became a symbol of this crazy market. We in the museums don't know what to do any more; how can we possibly buy any more paintings at such prices?'

'You've already got far too many: hundreds of thousands of pictures piled up in reserve in some damp place which is expensive for the taxpayer to maintain, and he doesn't even get to see them, though he still has to pay for the space. It's stuff which is forgotten whereas it could instead cheer up some drab office or home: it could circulate. Once something goes into a museum, it never comes out again: it dies,' said Huk. His long face looked like the face of an albino horse. He had never wished to acknowledge his own pederasty and had therefore nursed an imaginary passion for Maria Callas whom he had met just once and whom, according to his version, he had kissed with transport. He perspired as he talked and, when he talked of Maria Callas, he sweated profusely. Marina and R. remained silent. One of Marina's legs pressed against R.'s knees. She had traced the outline of her wide-open eyes in blue: it set off the dense colour of her irises.

'Come to Bratislava,' said Huk invitingly; those three words resounded like the title of some song. 'There's a performance on there which you just can't afford to miss.'

Was it a private performance or was it opera? wondered R. Was it the sort of show in which he might participate as an object or a subject? The tone of Vladislav Huk's suggestion had left him perplexed, full of doubt.

'Dauphine is in Prague,' whispered Valentina in Polissena's ear. 'Have you seen each other?'

'Dauphine?' queried Polissena with surprise. 'What's she doing here? I didn't summon her – she's certainly not here for me. No, quite the contrary, she ought to be in the Paris office. But she's Swiss: you can never trust a Swiss.'

'Above all, you should never trust Dauphine,' Valentina put in. Polissena looked at her uncomprehendingly. Was she trying to tell her something? Or maybe there was some rivalry between the two secretaries. In any case, she wanted to go back home with R.; she would talk of Dauphine some other time. 'Will you call me tomorrow?'

'For sure. I have to speak to you; there are things I must tell you – about the Caravaggio, I mean the Caravaggios . . .'

'What time can I call you?'

'No, I'll ring you.'

Conversation was flagging. R. had often wondered what on earth he was doing in such company and whether perhaps there were hidden meanings and allusions behind the words which he could not grasp. They drank a coffee in the square and then they all dispersed. Marian, Marina, Polissena and R. went home together.

She undressed him slowly: first his jacket, then his shirt, and his navy blue tie. She loved the way that R. dressed so conventionally. She removed his chastity belt. She wore a short skirt, gathered at the waist, and high-heeled shoes, but she had already taken off her silk blouse and liberated her breasts; R. kissed them every time she bent over him to remove one more item of clothing, to peel off a sock or untie a shoe.

They threw themselves at each other, seeking each other with their hands, their lips, their tongues, their knees, their feet. R. felt hard against her belly. She pressed her body against him, finding pleasure in every movement, rocking herself on one leg, stroking herself against him with the lips of her belly which swelled ever more open against R.'s legs, as if she wanted to be transfixed by those limbs also. They went on enjoying each other without yet taking one another, as he became heavier and heavier, and her legs trembled.

He delighted in the softness of Polissena's bosom; he looked for it with his lips, sucking the hardened nipples, playing with his lips around Polissena's thighs, where they are softest and at their most vulnerable, where they enclose the throbbing secret of the female body. She suddenly grasped him by the shoulders and forced him under her; she mounted him and sat astride his abdomen, pounding him into her. Swollen, rigid, tumescent, he disappeared into her as into an open mouth, a mouth which swallowed him up in one go, only to retreat again delicately. She rose and trotted on top of him, lowering herself on to him, looking at him all the while, staring at him. Then R. took

131

to clasping her down by his side, and then he took her from behind, forging between the lips of her sex, grasping her thighs between his hands and plunging himself ever more deeply into her. He pressed his firm legs against the mattress so as to gain a better purchase; Polissena could feel the muscles of his calves. She could feel her belly liquefying: she shuddered beneath his palpitating kiss which made her gasp and come. R. swelled up once more within her, outside her, at once, after only a few minutes.

Her eyes were still misty and her belly was still wet when the door opened and Marina appeared dressed in a transparent nightdress which hid neither her intentions nor her body. It was indeed splendid. Her high and heavy breasts fell from graceful shoulders over a minute waist; her hips widened like a vase over her perfectly black triangle, which looked inviting and mysterious.

Marina approached the single bed upon which both R. and Polissena lay piled up on one another, still panting. She kneeled beside them without speaking – she never spoke anyway – and gazed at them intently.

To start with, she fondled both of them; lightly, with delicacy, she caressed Polissena and massaged R.'s back; then she pressed the points around her groin with gentle stabbing movements and expert pressure.

Her arrival was unexpected and almost embarrassing given that R. was just about to doze off in the arms of his lover, overjoyed to be alone with her at long last. Polissena also wanted R. to be all hers that night, only hers. But R.

suspected that Marina's arrival had been planned with his lover's connivance.

Marina's head dropped slowly down Polissena in a repetitive movement, down towards the centre of her body. She inserted her other hand between her buttocks, which rose and then fell once more. Polissena was already swollen, stimulated and ready: she put up no resistance; she coiled around herself. She enjoyed herself more fully and more violently than when R. took her. He realized this and was almost embittered by the observation; he spied on her sullenly, perhaps offended in spite of himself. And now Marina began to stroke the still violet stripes of his scars, running her cheeks and tongue along the more colourful ones, along the grooves, as she promised – in the softest of murmurs – renewed violence.

As she whispered in Czech, she also swallowed R.'s spent member so that there issued from her mouth a string of incomprehensible words, distorted by the impediment of her vocal chords; it sounded like a strange litany. Whilst she continued to stroke Polissena, Marina now focused her attention on R., making sure not to graze him with her teeth, and R. grew within her small mouth. His muscular and slightly short legs brushed against her breasts; he plunged so far into her mouth that she felt nauseous.

He could feel that Polissena was still delighting in the alien touch of the intruder and, almost out of revenge, R. thrust himself against the girl's trachea, filling her throat and finding satisfaction in feeling Marina's fragile neck almost snapping under the impact. He was left stunned and exhausted.

'Now it's my turn,' said Marian aloud. He must have walked into the room without any of the three noticing; he stood watching them. R. turned towards him. 'Turn around,' ordered Marian.

As Marina nudged him to make him roll over on the mattress, R. suddenly understood that Marian wanted to make use of his body.

'No, I don't want to. We're no longer at the castle, and Polissena doesn't want me to either.'

'Tell him to do it,' ordered Marian, standing on his feet, exposed and naked. His swollen tension was poised in an erection; it pointed threateningly towards R.; his fleshy mouth, framed by that moustache, had a genital appearance. R. found him disgusting.

'Do it for me,' whispered Polissena in a docile tone. R. was astonished that his lover should ask this of him, that she should want to see him mounted by Marian. But maybe it was because she despised Marian that the sacrifice of R. would thereby seem that much more complete. R. looked at her apprehensively.

Marina was holding on to his arms as if to nail him down to the bed, to prepare him.

'Someone ought to go and fetch the whip,' said Marian. 'What, after all, were all those hours at Hloboke for? You've got to pack him off somewhere else. There's one in England where he'll learn to submit completely after only a few hours. Or else there's Tatiana: she transferred from Clapham to Venice – she's the best of the lot.'

'He really hasn't learnt to accept yet,' commented Marina. Only now did R. register that also Marina's buttocks were covered in purple stripes.

'We weren't expecting this,' said Polissena, as if excusing herself.

'But if you ask him to accept for your sake, he must accept,' suggested Marian.

'Don't ask me to,' asked R. instead.

'I won't ask it of you,' conceded Polissena.

Completely naked, Marian, whose pout twisted his lips in a still more obscene fashion, left the room in disappointment; he felt insulted.

'Let's sleep,' proposed Polissena to Marina who remained frozen in amazement beside their bed. Marina could not understand how R. had had the courage to rebel, to refuse.

'Aren't we even going to whip him?'

'Good night,' murmured Polissena.

'Just a tiny bit?'

III

The Grand Hotel at Bratislava (five-star category) had neither hot nor cold water. There was not even a bed in their room and, as R. leant over to grab a clothes-hanger, the only light bulb in the room crashed down on his head. They had decided not to go to the performance staged by Vladislav Huk after all, so they left most of their luggage in the boot of the car, and took only their washbags up to their room: they wanted to escape from Czechoslovakia as soon as possible. Polissena rang down to reception. 'Send me someone to mend the lamp, and we've got to have running water, else just what do you think you're up to flogging a room with bathroom at such a price? It's supposed to be a super luxury-class hotel! There isn't even a bed!'

A small basin slopping with lukewarm water arrived carried by a chambermaid who was obviously used to very different sorts of activity. The electrician followed. 'They're inefficient,' he confided. 'Look! By wedging the bugging device down here, they've short-circuited the whole system. They patched it up but the wire's still exposed. Look! It's like the electric chair at Sing Sing.'

He was a great big burly fellow with sagging cheeks like a spaniel.

'Listen, could you by any chance have a quick look at the bathroom as we're not getting a drop of water?'

'Oh, there's never any water in this hotel; in fact I don't think there ever has been. They put the pipes in the wrong way round. No thanks, don't give me a tip — I wouldn't know what to do with a korona. This country's the pits. And to think that poor old Bratislava isn't even Czech, at least not historically speaking.'

She had laid herself down; her silk blouse reached to just above her crotch. 'Christ, these made-up countries are just a disaster! Look at Lebanon: lots of different tribes strung together by hateful hypocrites sitting around some table thousands of miles away.'

136

R. did not know what Polissena was on about. History had never been his strong point, and at Eton they had only taught him English history anyway. He came to lie down beside her. 'I can't stand Marian,' he confessed. 'He's revoltingly effeminate with those swollen, over-red lips.'

'Yes, he's horrible.'

'Why d'you go on seeing him then?'

Polissena decided not to give him a direct answer. 'But if you really had accepted . . . you should have obeyed me . . . it would have been the way to make me understand that you're really mine, that you belong to me, that you're my object.'

'But I am your object,' R. anxiously reassured her.

'But you have to realize the pleasure of submission, of belonging to me even when we're not together, by means of others. What do you think about when I ask you to show your love for me? You shouldn't feel any rebellious urges: giving in should give you only pleasure.'

'That's just the way it is.'

'Are you sure?'

R. was meditating as he lay on his back staring at the ceiling. 'Who is this Tatiana person that Marian was referring to?'

'Don't you worry; I'd never send you to her.'

He continued staring at the ceiling. Maybe he should not ask her too many questions. 'Why do they want to foist the Caravaggio on to you?'

'Maybe they want to compromise me. They certainly want to get it out of Czechoslovakia without it being smuggled, and they want to get it on to the international market. Granted, the whole business is well planned, and the painting was stolen years ago, but the "Nativity" is still the last canvas painted by Caravaggio after Naples and Malta, when he was about to set off for Porto Ercole where he died.'

'How did that happen?'

'He died of malaria, of madness and despair, as he ran along the beach of La Feniglia trying to chase the ship which was sailing away full of his belongings and all his baggage. But what I was meaning to say is that this "Nativity" is very well known: from being a "scandalous" realist painter, Caravaggio became – in our eyes, at any rate – the first modern painter. From Roman master, having absorbed every influence, every school with which he came into contact, he became the painter who you could say invented the Spanish School. Rubens admired it, this last Caravaggio, and in the "Nativity" you can already detect Zurbarán and all the Spaniards. All to say, how the hell can you make believe that they're four new canvases? It's a catalogued work; it's a widely known fact that it was stolen and when. Chopping it up into four was just criminal.'

'Why don't you report them to the police?'

'Report whom? Marian would say that it was acquired by the Czech government. The only obvious thing is that I've got to steer well clear of it all, keep away as much from Marian as from the Caravaggio, or rather the Caravaggios.'

They took each other gently that night, and fled from the hotel early the next morning.

They had not yet cleared Bratislava when the road signs began to indicate the frontier. R. had not grasped that it was so close. The frontier effectively cut through the suburbs of the city. The markings for Vienna seemed to merge into the background, and the motorway was transformed into a little lane. Who, after all, would ever dream of crossing that frontier? The usual hostile landscape terrorized them: it looked like a scene from Berg – industrial quantities of barbed wire, searchlights which appeared as though they had been directly transplanted from a death camp which dazzled the hedges of the enclosures, the palings stuck into the minefields, the sirens which howled against a background of detonations. The roadblocks at the frontier were several: they spent hours looking for scraps of tissue paper, tracing receipts which the guards scrutinized with porcine, hostile, suspicious eyes. The guard, who was kitted out with mirrors to check whether some political refugee was hanging on to the chassis of the car, and kept his revolver and sub-machine-gun in full view, was followed by alsatian dogs. It seemed utterly dim of them to display so disarmingly the disagreeable character of their socialist republic.

Polissena had taken to reading a book: she might as well – they would spend at least another couple of hours in that godforsaken place.

It was the frontier guard with the deep blue eyes lost in the midst of too much flesh who found the Caravaggio in R.'s suitcase. 'Someone must have planted it there,' said R. in alarm.

'That's an old story,' replied the guard, looking into

his eyes, 'but I've never yet heard it told about such a sizeable object.'

'We left our suitcases in the car in Bratislava,' Polissena reminded him. 'They must have planted it in there during the night.'

'Honestly – I know absolutely nothing about it.' Could R. be involved in the plot? Might they have paid him? Polissena pondered the possibility for a moment. But R.'s blue eyes told the truth: there was no reason to suspect him and, in any case, R. would certainly not have hidden the picture inside his own suitcase. He would have used one of the suitcases of rather masculine design in brown leather which belonged to Polissena. 'Maybe Marian planted it . . .' R. suggested.

'It's quite likely,' she answered under her breath. 'Or Marina. Or one of my secretaries . . .' She thought of Valentina's words which she had not taken seriously enough at the time, after that dinner in Prague. What was Dauphine up to in Czechoslovakia? Why did Valentina want to talk to her in private? 'Now we've got to get ourselves out of this mess.'

It was not going to be easy.

They found themselves in a dark room which gave on to two latrine doors: these filled the room with a penetrating stench.

'What a stink!' exclaimed Polissena.

'Colonel, sir, this British citizen's under arrest,' declared the man in uniform surrounded by the whiff of ammonia. Gesturing in R.'s direction, he communicated with a man in civilian clothes who was sitting at the large, untidy, roughly hewn writing table and who, in order not to mar the Kafkaesque nature of the situation, was filling in some flimsy sheets of paper with figures and numbers.

Polissena went to sit down in front of him, intending to seduce him with her smiles and gestures. 'There's clearly a misunderstanding . . . Would it be all right if we telephone Marian Svoboda of the People's Gallery of Prague?'

Two guards — one of whom was the one who had declared R. under arrest — left the smelly passage and did not reappear for some twenty minutes. They whispered alternately and at great length into the ear of the colonel in mufti; it was an utterly pointless precaution as neither R. nor Polissena would have understood what they were saying anyway, and then they retired into the foetid obscurity of the background.

'Comrade Professor Svoboda says he knows nothing of such a canvas. But he confirms that he is acquainted with the lady, and is surprised at what has happened.'

R. feared that Polissena would abandon him: she could have claimed that, since the canvas was in R.'s suitcase and not in her own, she knew nothing about the picture.

'What have you got to say about all this, Madame Braganza?' continued the Colonel from the secret services; 'Comrade Svoboda gave us an important piece of information: he tells me I'm sitting in front of the director of the Louvre Museum.'

Polissena could disown him, thought R.; he would end up in Spillberg, in Brno.

'I love you,' she said to him as if to reassure him, as if she had understood exactly what R. was thinking.

But it was the unexpected arrival of Baron von Wurzburg together with his new lover, a young Czech by the name of Proko Martinu, and followed by a pair of sausage dogs which immediately started quarrelling with the border alsatians, which saved Polissena. It was a peculiar coincidence, as the Baron never usually travelled by car: he deemed it excessively slow and uncomfortable. His private airplane and his two helicopters – lavishly done up by David Mlinario – ferried him to all the music festivals.

'Hans-Herbert!' exclaimed Polissena in surprise.

'The Baron von Wurzburg!' echoed R.

As both famous collector and powerful ally of the Czech government, the Baron would stand surety for them. He looked at the canvas picked out of R.'s suitcase; he said that it was a worthless copy and tucked it under his arm. He too travelled with a souvenir of Czechoslovakia. He showed off three modern pictures painted in tempera depicting views of Prague: the castle, the Moldava and the Sanctuary of Loreto above Prague; he carried with him a receipt to vouch for the piddling value of the three works – but he liked them nonetheless, he added. Polissena, on the other hand, found them very ugly: how could Hans-Herbert, a man of such taste, bring home such rubbish? Excusing himself with the border guards, Proko explained that the Baron was in a hurry; he had agreed to a loan of part of his collection for an exhibition in Leningrad and another in Prague; and that very night, the Baron had a dinner engagement with Herbert von Karajan. The following day, they were going to see *Carmen*.

This information seemed to be of great interest to the border guards and the secret service agents locked into the malodorous room. In this way, they could fantasize about an evening of luxury, about the refined meals, the sparkling performance.

Out of the Baron's pocket – it was right next to him – Proko extracted two small wads of green paper bound with elastic and, there and then, without any embarrassment, he inserted one into the pocket of the guard who had first arrested R. He laid the slimmer package of much more exciting denominations on the table. 'Perhaps you could distribute these, Colonel.'

The four of them left the stinking room; Polissena and R. were amazed but delighted to leave that country with all its attendant dangers; they were followed by the Baron and Proko, with the sausage dogs bringing up the rear.

Over on the other side, in Austrian territory, the Baron's private helicopter was waiting for them. Polissena picked it out by the coat of arms of the von Wurzburgs painted on the fuselage.

Proko nodded to the chauffeur. 'You head for Munich.'

'I just don't know how to thank you!' said Polissena.

'Don't mention it,' replied the Baron.

'Thanks very much!' exclaimed R.

'Don't mention it.'

And they walked towards the helicopter as their Buick proceeded in the direction of Munich.

That was how the Caravaggio crossed the Czech border.

IV

The following day, after calling the office and sending off
a few telexes, they caught the first plane leaving Vienna
for Paris: Louis would come and fetch them from the airport
with Dauphine. 'I don't understand why they planted it in
your suitcase,' she remarked as she sipped a glass of mineral
water – she never drank champagne when flying.

'They obviously got it wrong. Your suitcases have a
masculine look about them – but it's clear who's responsible
for putting it there.'

'If it was Marian, then it must have been planned by
the Czech secret service, but what could they possibly want
from me? If they wanted to blackmail me or get me into
trouble, they would use the photographs which they must
have of you, me, Marian, Marina and so on, taken from
above, below, side on, with telephoto lens and microscope,
in colour and black and white, enlarged . . . And besides,
Marian couldn't have predicted that once we got to Bratislava, we wouldn't have taken our baggage up to the hotel
bedroom. That means that if we'd gone to the performance
staged by Vladislav Huk the other night and you'd decided
to change, you would have discovered the canvas before we
ever crossed the frontier.'

'You mean they planted it on me when we were in
Bratislava?'

'Of course – without realizing that that was your suitcase and not mine. Or maybe they did it right at the

frontier, like they do with heroin. If they want to take you in, they have this nasty habit of planting some in your pocket and then arresting you, claiming to have discovered it on you, and then there's nothing you can do.'

'It's not worth travelling to those kinds of places.'

'No; they kick you black and blue and then force you to "confess".'

'Really?' Such notions were too far removed from the tranquillity of Monpleasance. 'Has it ever happened to you?'

'No, being a museum director means you don't get in anyone's way.'

'Well, you must've got in someone's way this time,' R. reminded her; 'either because you refused to hand me over to Marian or because you didn't want to have anything to do with the Caravaggio.'

'Maybe there's more to it: there's probably more to follow, that worries me. Do you love me?'

'You won't leave me?'

Polissena looked into R.'s eyes: they seemed weighed down by his lashes; she contemplated the beauty of his face once more. 'I love you so much it's killing me.'

'Well, that's another matter.'

'No, it's important; I like to look at you and touch you and have you touch me.'

'I'm your object,' R. whispered in her ear, his voice brimming with pleasure.

'I like to see you taken by others but I also want you to be taken by me. I love you passionately: will you always let me enjoy you by profaning your body and by seeing you cower beneath the blows of others?' Polissena gazed into his eyes, then into his mouth, his teeth, his ears.

'Sometimes I'm afraid that you have other "88s", other keys, other chastity belts.'

'No. There's only you.'

The airplane landed at Charles de Gaulle slightly ahead of schedule. They had just dozed off uncomfortably.

The airport throbbed with fake modernism: a *Star Trek* style redolent of the sixties, a kind of home-made *2001*. Feeling somewhat ridiculous, they progressed along the travolator which bore passengers to the central node of the airport and was lined by great illuminated sunflowers flashing advertising slogans such as:

LUI – THE FRAGRANCE FOR HIM FOR THEM

Le Cadet – depilatory lotion for men

There was Puledro and Kouros too, aftershaves both of them. A vigorous and striking young man pictured on the inviting suspended lollipops flaunted the new make-up for men.

POUR L'HOMME
nourishing cream for the masculine complexion

as well as

BROSSE
Hair loss? Say goodbye to baldness anxiety with BROSSE

'Would you still love me if I were bald?' he asked

her, turning towards her between one plastic sunflower and another.

'Not a bit,' replied Polissena; 'I find bald men repulsive.' She did not like hairy men either, she added. She pondered for a moment. 'Ever since they discovered that it was us who bought you stuff, they've bombarded us with advertising. At least we know what to get you for Christmas though.'

'What's it to be then?'

'Scents and baubles.'

'What about all the things we used to buy for you?'

'You certainly never bought me any. And when the hell have men ever smothered their wives with flowers or jewels? It only ever happens to whores, or in films.'

Perhaps she minded that R. had never sent her flowers . . . In effect, yes, she did mind: it had never even entered his head . . . Too bad . . . you couldn't have everything. Either an object or a master who sent you flowers, and perhaps not even that. She preferred an object.

Her hair was elaborately dressed. Dauphine de Brantes was waiting for them. Her make-up was carefully smoothed and shined on her skin. It was too shiny. Tall, with a silk Hermès scarf, a well-cut jacket, not beautiful, but skilfully put together, with her impeccable leather trimmings from Ferragamo, she was covered in expensive things, all gleaming and soft.

'Ah! Well done, Dauphine!'

'Good morning, Madame!' She smiled. She was carrying a pile of newspapers on her arm; they were so heavy that they almost overwhelmed her.

'Good morning, Mr Reading. Did you have a pleasant journey?'

She was the perfect secretary.

'What's new?' asked Polissena.

'Several urgent calls from Monsieur Newman, and from Mr Lockhart who's at Cranlie Hall till midday. Also from the Marchioness of Beckford who asks if you know of the whereabouts of her son. And a call from the Minister: he wants an explanation for the Caravaggio story ... it's reported in some of the newspapers – I bought them all. I also bought the new weeklies and monthlies for Monsieur.'

'For me?'

'They're the new magazines for men. Have a look. *Pour l'Homme* has just come out – it's a monthly devoted to masculine art and culture. Then there's *He*, a men's fashion weekly, and *Voilà les Mâles!* an excellent biweekly. If you're after some juicy gossip, there's *Le goût masculin* or *Culture virile*. But I prefer *Kingman*: it's got special features on gymnastics: how to broaden your chest, and hints on how to, well, you know what I mean ...' The plastic advertising images dangling on their rods continued to flash past.

'I'm afraid I don't speak any French ...' R. excused himself.

'You can look at the pictures then – there's so little text anyway.'

'Do you read them then, Dauphine?' asked Polissena with interest. But her mind was clearly miles away. How did the story about the Caravaggio discovered at the border make the newspapers? There was no one at the Czech border apart from . . . 'But you, Dauphine, weren't you in Czechoslovakia?'

'Me? No, I never left Paris. There was loads to do in the office and then, when this story about the Caravaggio broke, I had to field endless calls from the press; I told them that I knew nothing and that you were still abroad . . .'

'But Valentina told me . . .' Polissena decided to drop the subject.

Louis smiled at them both, and bowed very slightly to R. as well. He slipped behind them and opened the door of the Mercedes. 'The coffee's in the thermos flask, Madame,' he hinted.

'What do the papers say?' Polissena asked Dauphine once she was comfortably positioned amidst the cushions and smells of the car.

'That you and your companion – they don't name names – were crossing the Czech border with a Caravaggio in your luggage, which was probably heading for the Louvre,' Dauphine replied.

'A genuine Caravaggio?'

'They don't say.'

'I wonder who wants to land me in the shit,' Polissena muttered to herself; she went on frowning beneath her black curls for the rest of the trip back from Charles de Gaulle to Paris.

She swiftly leafed through the newspapers, pausing at those pages marked in red ink whilst R. looked at the glossies devoted to men's beauty. There were a few in English, like *Snippet* about the new hairstyles, or *Golf and*

Bowls, a monthly for the sporting gentleman. And *Cole*: the title referred to Cole Porter, rather than Coca-Cola; it played on the nostalgic theme of transatlantic homosexuality thirties-style, Lucky Luciano at the races and such like, whereas *Voici les Garçons* presented the new collection '*pour l'homme d'affaires et des loisirs*'. What was she going to do with R. when she was out at the office? Polissena smeared some colour on her lips and tried to relax. 'What d'you want to do for the rest of the morning? Do you want to see the Musée d'Orsay?'

'What?' asked R., whose blue eyes were glued to a photograph of a platinum chain poised on a very hairy chest.

'It was once the Orsay station and now it's been converted into a wonderful museum.'

'I'm not that wild about museums.'

Thank God. There was nothing wrong with not being interested in museums. On the contrary. Museums, exhibitions, culture: it was a current obsession. 'What about the Picasso museum?'

R. was still studying his glossies.

'Or would you prefer to do some shopping? I could tell Louis to drop you off on the Faubourg St Honoré after he's left me at the office. Here are the house keys: Dauphine has a set too, so don't be alarmed if she comes in. Or the cleaning lady, though she hardly ever turns up. You could visit some of those exquisite shops, or go to the barber – Monsieur Elysée or else Le Lion: they're supposed to be good. And then there are all those boutiques – Monsieur

Dior, Monsieur Cardin: he's even taken to signing lavatory paper. You could get some lunch at Gargantua which is near the church of S. Roc and take it home. Then come and pick me up at the office in the afternoon after you've had a look at the glass pyramid.'

'What glass pyramid?'

'The one in the courtyard of the Louvre.'

'It's years since I was last in Paris . . .'

'But you must have read about it in the papers. When it was inaugurated by Mitterrand there wasn't anything to inaugurate as it wasn't yet finished . . .'

'I ought to telephone my mother,' said R. looking at Polissena as she removed her glasses. The mere fact of wearing them, reflected R., underlined that she was older than him; by how much, he did not know. He had tried to find out from her passport. Perhaps he should not even wonder how old his mistress was; maybe he was thus committing some sin: it was a form of criticism after all.

'You can do that from my apartment.'

There was a small pile of mail under all the newspapers.

'I only brought the letters which looked most urgent,' explained Dauphine, her wavy blonde hair slightly ruffled by the wind. Dauphine opened all of Madame's letters as a matter of course.

They were passing by the Abbey of S. Denis. 'The kings of France are buried there,' Polissena pointed out; she liked guiding, educating; 'but only the more important, the more stylish ones. We'll go there some time,' she promised.

151

R. raised his large eyelids from the sheaves of paper towards the suburbs of Paris.

'But that's . . . yes, yes . . . I recognize that . . .' He was looking the other way where, white and monstrous, loomed the Sacré Coeur of Montmartre.

'We're invited by the Count and Countess of Polignac-Hérisson this evening,' she notified him.

'What, me too?' R. caught a glimpse of the invitation. It bore the words Madame Braganza Lockhart and guest.

'Yes, you too.'

'Who are these people?'

'Rich collectors. He – Benedict – known as Héri, as in Hérisson – he looks like one too – inherited factories, ports, steelworks and a penchant for opium from his mother. His grandfather was Japanese. It's not done to delve too deeply into his background. In any case, he's just remarried.'

'How old is he?' asked R. That kind of chronicle always fascinated him.

'He's a man who only ever marries prostitutes,' Polissena went on without answering R.'s question. 'This must be his sixth . . . how old is he? About seventy, but he carries it well, like all rich people. He's got a sensational collection of paintings, though some of them have been over-restored. There's a bit of everything in it, too much of everything.'

'What's wrong with that?'

'A private collection ought to express the taste and inspiration of a great man, and this Hérisson is not a great man, though he thinks he is because he's loaded with money and opium and because, since he's rich, everybody tells him he's a great man.'

'What'll it be like this evening?'

'Superb: caviar, wife number six, paintings. Don't worry: you'll have a good time.'

R. wandered around Paris. He minded not knowing a single word of the language, especially as a whole succession of schools and private tutors had done all they could to instil it in him, but his memory declined to reproduce the slightest word or phrase.

As Louis dropped off R.'s luggage in Polissena's apartment on the Rue de Lille, R. walked through the streets looking at the shop windows and thinking about the two of them. Maybe it was a mistake to do so, seeing as Polissena seemed to deny him all future prospects, and even ignored them, treating him like some kind of jewel, something which she could quite easily have done without. The idea that he might lose his lover hit him at the base of his stomach: she might drop him there and then, telling him that she had too much to do at the office that day; she might send him Louis to accompany him on his shopping spree, whilst she went off, leaving him behind.

V

At the office, Polissena found a long list of people all urgently requiring her to call them; Valentina Bulova's name was also on the list. Her message had arrived as Polissena was on her way in from the airport: she recorded that she had already tried to catch up with her several times and that she urgently needed to speak to her.

'Did Valentina call for me?' Polissena again asked Dauphine.

'No, I never heard from her.'

Now Polissena was certain that Dauphine was lying.

Oliver rang a few minutes later. 'We've got it!'

'What's that?'

'Caravaggio's Madonna – we haven't yet had a look at her, but we've got proof that she's the genuine article.'

'Who did you buy her off? Where is she?'

'I don't know where she is; you're the one who ought to know that. After all, you brought her out of Czechoslovakia. There are three others.'

'I didn't smuggle out three other Caravaggios.'

'How's that? Weren't you the one who discovered them?' There was a vindictive edge to her husband's voice; his innate male superiority and Etonian arrogance had always been offended by the high esteem in which his wife was generally held, and by her status and her job. He had always endeavoured to demolish her self-confidence.

'I know nothing about this Caravaggio – or rather, these Caravaggios.'

'The consortium is expecting a signed authentication from you which will be printed in our brochure. That's why I'm phoning. The company's going public and the more bona fide authentications we can get our hands on, the better it'll be. You've also got to confirm that we snatched it from the hands of the Louvre.'

'That's not true for a start, and what's more I don't want to lose my job.'

'But just think of the money we'll make with four Caravaggios! I mean, too bad if you lose your job.'

'Money gets frittered away, but my job is priceless.'

'Well, you'd better wave it goodbye then.'

Maybe it was him, Oliver, who had set the snare in order to appropriate her prestige and her superiority for himself. 'Is our cousin with you?' he went on in a voice which quivered with fake indifference.

Yes, it must have been him – he had taken his revenge in all sorts of ways.

'I left a message at Rue de Lille,' he added; 'you've got to go to Eton to see Boy: he wants to see you for some reason best known to himself, and I simply don't have the time to go down there.'

'But you're there . . . and I'm in deep trouble at the moment.'

'I'm calling from the country and then there's the Caravaggio business, the consortium . . . the company's called Caravaggio Masterpieces Ltd. I really haven't got time for him . . .'

Boy was their youngest son. What irritated Polissena most was that in public Oliver pretended to be the perfect parent. But for Oliver, children were only social attributes. Suddenly it dawned on her that Oliver's message at Rue de Lille was not there: she had listened to all of them.

From inside her adjacent office Dauphine called out, 'Oh! I forgot to tell you that your husband left a message about your son – you're meant to go and see him at the school.'

'Did he call the office?'

'Yes. I spoke to him.'

She was lying again. Oliver had specified that he had left a message on her answering machine at Rue de Lille.

The telephone conversation with the Minister was very brief. It was also disagreeable. It was not to his liking that a government official should be mixed up in some swindle which threatened to blow up into a scandal, he said drily. She should justify herself and clarify the situation. Polissena replied by saying that she did not know how the Caravaggio had ended up in her friend's suitcase; she did not know where it was at the moment, and she did not understand how her husband could have obtained it. Yes, it was true that Oliver Lockhart of Caravaggio Masterpieces Ltd was her husband. As for the other Caravaggios which had been publicized, Polissena had never laid eyes on them, and she had no desire to see them either.

The Minister had not believed her. 'Don't forget that civil servants tend to resign if matters remain unclear,' he had concluded angrily. Even when they were up to their necks in it, politicians never resigned, mused Polissena; civil servants not only had to be honest, they had to flaunt it too.

Meanwhile R. had reached Rue de Lille and pressed the button on the front door. Any old thief with the slightest knowledge of French history could have penetrated the private porches of most Parisian homes. If the secret code which had to be keyed in did not coincide with the date of the Paris Commune, then it matched the year of the French Revolution. The passage opened on to an elegantly grey courtyard. The wooden fixtures and casings were painted in that handsome dark green which is dear to Parisians; on the right, Polissena's apartment rose up on two floors.

He turned the key. The wooden internal staircase was decorated in a fishing motif or, rather, it was adorned with all sorts of fish and fishermen: ceramic dolphins, tiles depicting monkfish, sea bream and sea bass and red mullet. There were vases ornate with octopus, mussels and oysters, langoustines and scallops, lobsters and cuttlefish, nets and rods. There were photographs and pictures of the sturgeon and pearl and shellfish fishermen of yesteryear.

R. was taken aback by the decor; he had never seen anything of the kind before. He was speechless. What would his mother the marchioness have said?

The fish flooded into the drawing room which was entirely painted in aquatic motifs, whilst the bedroom was neo-gothic and sinister. A screen divided it from the bathroom; Polissena had made the wardrobes from two confession boxes, and the bathtub was wedged into a catafalque. The walls — even those of the bathroom — were crammed with images of monks condemning naked and penitent women, ready to do anything for the sake of gaining admission to the Kingdom of Heaven. There were skeletons sharing the favours of a buxom lady of Rubenesque form, between themselves, and also various memento mori. Such curious things had never been seen at Monpleas-ance. Apart from its weirdness, the apartment possessed that singular tidiness of a home inhabited by one person alone, a bachelor who does not tolerate the presence of another. The orderly arrangement was almost suffocating and every cupboard appeared to conceal some electronic gadget in impeccable working order. There were no family photographs in the house, no trinkets. R. profaned it immediately by abandoning his shoes by the sofa and not replacing the loo-paper in its frog-shaped basket. He took a bath, leaving a dark and hairy ring on the enamel tub which was bound to infuriate whoever had to clean it. Polissena would take note of everything with ill-concealed irritation.

R. lay down on her bed – the headboard was carved in the design of a spider's web: it was the work of Matta – and he telephoned Monpleasance. His mother had gone out and his sisters were out riding, but his father was in.

'Just ringing to tell you I'm fine; I'm in Paris.'

'You're in Paris? How's that?'

'That's how it worked out.'

'You never asked my leave . . . when did you go? I hadn't actually realized you'd gone.'

'Well, Mama did because she called Cousin Polissena Lockhart to find out.'

'Who?'

'Cousin Oliver's wife, Polissena Lockhart.'

'Never heard of her.'

He gave up. He signed off and fell asleep. It was

perhaps twenty minutes later that he was awakened by a rustling sound, someone else's presence. He observed Dauphine moving about the writing table in the living room. She was standing next to the telephone and clearly did not expect to see R. 'Ah! Is that you?' she asked nervously, in some embarrassment.

'What are you doing here, Dauphine?'

'I was listening to the messages recorded during Madame's absence.' But she was actually deleting them instead.

VI

As they drove across Paris with Louis impassively intent at the steering wheel (the Polignac-Hérissons lived in Neuilly), it struck him once more that Polissena was worried; under those dark curls, her forehead was still creased.

'Dauphine came home today,' he informed her. 'She seemed to be wiping off your telephone messages and didn't expect to see me. She was rather embarrassed.'

Polissena was beginning to understand what was going on. She had not yet been able to catch up with Valentina who was obviously trying to warn her.

That evening Polissena was dressed in black, in a short slip which made her thin legs look longer, though it did not flatter the colour of her skin. She had applied some dark lipstick to her mouth and two rubies hung from her ears. 'They're fake,' she told him when she saw R.'s big blue eyes alight admiringly on her lobes. 'Whereas those of Countess Hérisson – Katiusha – might look fake, but they're sure to be genuine.'

Katiusha Polignac-Hérisson was not yet ready when R. and Polissena stepped into the extremely luxurious house. But then again, they were slightly early.

However, two hours later the Countess still had not come down as, tipsy and slobbering, Héri was still greeting his guests, declaring to all and sundry that he did not know them, even though there were famous names from the world of theatre, high finance and art amongst them.

'He's sloshed,' whispered Milagros Gautier who had sold him a notorious quantity of paintings and whom Héri had never yet succeeded in recognizing. Instead the Count had leapt towards R. whom he had never before seen in his life, mistaking him for his sister.

His rival collector, Baron von Wurzburg, was huddled under a pair of Matisses.

'Hans-Herbert, could you possibly explain this story to me?' asked Polissena at once. 'How come you were at the frontier, and where did you take the painting?'

'I recognized him.'

'Who?'

'From his armbands.'

'What were you doing on the Czech border?'

'Isn't he eight-eight?'

'How did the Caravaggio story get into the newspapers

the very next day if those present were just us and the officials you bribed? Can you explain that to me?' she insisted. 'And how come there are three other Caravaggios, I mean the three missing portions? And how did they come out and where are they now?'

'There's nothing to explain,' the Baron jerked away, apparently bored.

Was it him?

'Is it 88 from Hloboke? You were in trouble, and I always give my friends a helping hand if I can.'

'But you had your wad of dollars at the ready,' pursued Polissena.

'In Czechoslovakia, and Brazil, too, for that matter, you've always got to have various wads in your pocket.'

'And from what I've heard, the Caravaggio, the Caravaggios have been bought up by a group in the City.'

'Your husband bought them in association with a consortium, Caravaggio Masterpieces Ltd. Dauphine organized it all. All I'm after is a single section.'

'Dauphine?'

'I've simply got to have one: Héri's got two – even if they are over-restored – but the one my father left me is a fake. I want the angel with the Gloria in Excelsis Deo. Have you seen it, Polissena? The beauty of it! All I'm asking is to be able to buy the painting, the angel, the dark-haired youth . . . I've always wanted a Caravaggio . . .'

'But why d'you want to land me in the soup?'

'Me? What have I got to do with it? But tell me, that's eighty-eight . . . and as for that horrible Hérisson woman giving herself airs because she's got two Caravaggios and I've none . . .' There had always been rivalry between the two collectors. 'This opium-addled idiot's married the nth tart. And when they sit them beside you, you've just got to put up with them, with their conversation fit for Duchesses; they tell you they're the ones who choose the great pictures, the Manets and Monets which they still manage to confuse, and the Simone Martinis which they'd never heard about until a few months ago. I mean, just look at the taste of this place; aside from the paintings, it looks like a brothel . . . How does Héri do it? All that opium has clouded his faculties. God knows what those two get up to in bed. Otherwise he wouldn't have married her, that prostitute. She must suck him all over, I suppose; what do you think, Polissena? She probably sticks little creatures inside him . . . and then at dinner they tell you they read Proust and went to school at the Sacred Heart . . . But isn't he from Hloboke?'

From the other end of the drawing room, R. was apparently unable to free his gaze from the sinuous curves of the hostess. He could not take his eyes off the milky white breasts of Katiusha Polignac-Hérisson; they were boldly offered towards the ceiling, soft and exposed in a décolletage which revealed the deep and inviting cleavage of two worlds marvellously adorned with splendid sapphires.

'Haven't we already met?' Nicholas Newman asked him, nudging him with his elbow and interrupting the spell under which R. had fallen. 'Us two? eh? What's that? Yes, of course, with Madame Braganza at the restaurant, eh? I mean, well, what a memory! Reading, aren't you? eh? from Monpleasance. I'm right, aren't I?'

R. had finally met someone he knew. He looked at him, grateful at having been recognized.

'Where's Polissena? I have to talk to her. What's this absurd story about a Caravaggio? I read she had it in her suitcase, the Prague Caravaggio. What kind of a joke is this? Did you know that up till a few years ago Countess Polignac-Hérisson lived in a brothel, and now she wants to be a duchess? The Duchess of Las Ramblas! Lord knows how many times she had Las Ramblas when she lived in Spain; in and out, eh! eh! Not dell'Alhambra, but de las Ramblas!'

'Really?' R. could not follow such a volley of facts.

'Are you staying for the auction?'

'What?'

'Katiusha, the duchess, eh? eh! She's announced an auction in aid of charity. Everything's done for charity these days – galas, balls, operas, auctions. It's one way of climbing up the social ladder. But once you've scaled every rung, what d'you do next? Where are you then?'

The auction was not doing well. Katiusha had declared that the two lapdogs the size of mice were also on sale, along with eight pearls, a manuscript and seven Fortuny dresses. But those people already had everything: they were already bored with everything. So Katiusha contrived that some of those present should also be put up for auction. Robert Redford and the painter Valerio Adami, and the writer Maurice Rheims were knocked down for $20,000, but no lady had the courage to come forward and claim her due.

VII

Already from the bridge, from which rose up the most harmonious profile of the gothic chapel and the ancient nucleus of red brick, she could pick out the little boys dressed in black. Their black tails flapped elegantly around their small legs; their skin shone over-white, and their rigid collars stood out beneath the grey bags under their eyes; they were captive spirits. Boy also admitted that he felt himself a prisoner at Eton. In fact, the school stopped him from leaving the grounds at weekends, and discouraged communication with his family: not just letters, but also all those interests which were not closely tied to those of the college; they seemed only to be keen on subjects like music, biology, rowing and homosexuality.

Why on earth had Boy called her? Or had it been Master, or maybe Margot, the Dame who looked after the boys and the House? She could not understand it. The Housemaster never usually wanted to speak to parents, mothers in particular; he deemed them seriously stupid and unpleasant.

Polissena knew that she was not a good mother, but given that Oliver was appreciably worse as a parent, she felt that it was better not to heighten the emotional imbalance. The both of them might as well be inadequate parents; in any case, boys always ended up rebelling.

Boy's window gave on to the Victorian courtyard, but Polissena decided to go at once to the Housemaster who was bound to be free at that time of day. He was responsible for Boy's House and was consequently in charge of him. A teacher of history, a first-class mind, perhaps a trifle neurotic, the Housemaster was surrounded by little boys whom he desired but could not touch. Those poor little things already had to fight off the PE master who fondled them whenever he got the chance, and the divinity tutor too. Blessed are the Jews! Rabbis tended never to be homosexual, though admittedly being Jewish at Eton was a calamity; 'Jew' was a term of abuse here.

Boy did not talk much; he was visibly unhappy, not only because of his parents, but also because of his school, because he ate what he did and because he had to face up to a daily routine which depressed him.

But Polissena did not find George, the Housemaster, in his study, so she walked down the length of The Rigours looking for Margot. She found her in her quarters; she sprang out of the easy-chair into which she had huddled, only to sink back heavily into it.

'Good morning, Margot!'

At The Rigours, everybody called everybody else by their Christian name even if Polissena did not like the practice one bit, especially when she heard her beautiful name mutilated.

'Did you call me?' Margot responded with a boozy

complaint. 'Your son never eats at table . . .'

'But I trust he's behaving well.' Polissena cut her short; she wanted to take her leave from Margot as quickly as possible in view of the sherry fumes wafting around the small room; it was like being in a tavern since the bottle which Margot had swiftly hidden behind her armchair had fallen over and was spilling what remained of its contents on to the flowery carpet. 'But was it you who summoned me, Miss Lewisham?' insisted Polissena.

Margot's flesh was ruddy and creased, and her small ears were of course pierced at the lobe. Her hair was crinkled by a faulty perm which stopped short at the neck, Margot's voice was of the sort which is ashamed of its accent, so that every intonation was deliberately corrected and distorted in the manner of the pursed aristocratic mouths of the college inmates who teased the roundabout expressions favoured by Margot Lewisham, otherwise known as Dame Sherry.

She wore a pink angora jersey which stretched over her hips and sagging bosom, this last feature being a particular target for derision on the part of the forty inmates of The Rigours. She was meant to look after them; Margot was paid and lodged at Eton for that reason, but even when she was sober, she lacked the necessary abilities as well as the right ideas. Boy, for instance, had told his mother that when he had been sick in bed with fever, Margot had given him sixteen aspirin. On that occasion, Polissena had called Master Twitch: 'George! It's enough to poison the system!' From the depths of his soul, George Twitch, who specialized in the Georgian and Edwardian eras (he knew nothing of the rest: what was not strictly British history was beneath consideration), despised all women. It was therefore obvious that Margot, being ugly and drunken, had been selected as a post-maternal example which the boys would absorb; it was an almost assured method of directing them towards a homosexual vocation. In any case, all mothers were meant to understand that, once at The Rigours, the boys were not to be disturbed by telephone calls or letters. Master George was even more hostile to the idea of their coming to visit the boys: the school was supposed to replace the family, especially when the school happened to be Eton. Moreover, being an essentially female construct, the family was a fundamentally mistaken institution.

Whilst Margot was still collapsed into her easy-chair and Polissena was about to leave, the silence was ruptured by a hiccup which might equally have been a belch. Overcome by embarrassment, Margot pretended to have coughed.

'I'd better find George,' said Polissena as she fled from the room fragrant with the whiff of oloroso.

'Tell Boy that it would be better if I kept his money for him, otherwise he spends it all on food and eats it outside mealtimes,' she shouted from behind.

Polissena cut her short; 'Yes, yes,' she said, slamming the door; Margot would have spent the money on sherry in the same way that she already squandered the housekeeping funds.

She went down the narrow staircase from which emanated that unmistakable smell of English schools as well as hospitals: the smell of disinfectant mixed with sweat and animal fat fried many times over. She walked through the refectory of The Rigours, the walls of which were impregnated with the smell of boiled mutton, and up the beautiful Georgian staircase which led to Master George's private study.

The Master was alone; embarrassed at finding himself in female company, he became particularly irritable. His body unleashed itself in a couple of contractions. Extremely thin, his eyes magnified by the thick lenses of his spectacles, he shouted with false and exaggerated enthusiasm: 'Polissena!'

Out of fake familiarity they were all supposed to address each other by name and in deafeningly loud exclamations.

Nervous and fidgety, he offered her a cup of tea, knocking the spoon against the porcelain as he did so. He gave the chair a sharp tug.

'How's my son getting on?' asked Polissena at once so as not to prolong unnecessarily the torture provoked by her presence.

'He's not been very respectful; he announced that the food was terrible and refused to touch what he was served.'

'And what was so wrong with it?'

'What's more, he asked his friends to do the same too, to go on strike with him.'

'A hunger strike just like Gandhi?' She liked that; Polissena knew her son only slightly, but she found that this disclosure enabled her to admire the merits of her little Boy.

'That's just it,' answered Master Twitch, a couple of spasms rippling through his waistcoat. Polissena feared that these spasmodic movements would cause the tray with the teapot, the sugar-bowl and the fine Wedgwood cups to end up in smithereens on the floor. 'He's a boy who doesn't want to be like all the others, who refuses to adapt; he's on his own too much.'

'He cries often, that much I do know.'

'Everyone cries here: it's good to have a little cry some-times. Discipline is all about being sad, learning to cope with it. He's getting used to being away from his family.' He made an agitated movement. 'It would be better if you didn't make your presence known to him today, otherwise he'll be even more miserable when you take off again.'

'But I came on purpose to see him. Or to see you. Did you call me here?'

'No. Mothers have a disastrous influence on their sons.'

Polissena considered that she had had far too little influence on her children, and she feigned not to notice the latest muscular spasm which had contorted Master George's entire face. She said, 'Was it for this that you had me come here?'

'I did not ask to see you, Polissena.'

Then it was Boy who wished to speak to her, concluded Polissena. 'The boys say that Margot . . .'

'She's perfectly suitable,' George cut in and, glancing at the clock, he invited her to go. 'It's almost time for dinner.'

It was six in the afternoon.

She went out by the courtyard of The Rigours and was just about to slip into the staircase leading to the tiny cubicle where Boy lived when Valentina Bulova emerged from a red Fiesta.

'What are you doing here?' asked Polissena, looking pleased to see her.

'I was the one who asked you to come up to Eton, Madame. I needed to talk to you and it was the only way to get round Dauphine and your husband. I left the message that Boy required your presence; I knew that your husband would not have concerned himself about it. I didn't want to arouse any suspicions.'

'What do you mean, suspicions?'

'Let's go to your son's room – no one will disturb us there.'

'One of the best things about this school is the silence, the solitude and privacy of the place, just like a monastery . . .'

Polissena preceded her up the small wooden staircase. Boy's room was empty and decorated with posters and drawings from floor to ceiling. But it resounded with ear-splitting noise: from one side blared pop music, whilst from the other came jazz.

'I left you various messages, but I reckon Dauphine didn't let a single one through.'

At that moment, a swaying Margot burst into the tiny room. 'What? Two women?' she exclaimed in horror.

'We just met . . . I'm waiting for my son . . .'

'You want to see your son? Why's that?'

As Margot shut the door behind her, Polissena pursued the point. 'And then what?'

'Your husband is part of the set-up, and so is Dauphine. They threatened me and even went as far as to offer me a percentage of the shares . . .'

'What for?'

'To keep quiet.' Valentina smoothed a hand over her hair which formed a kind of broad crest on top of her head. Her lips were fleshy and her skin was white. 'As you know, your husband started up a consortium with some crooks from the City, and Dauphine and Monsignor Venini too, and together they bought the Caravaggios from the Czech government through Marian. Baron von Wurzburg wants one for his collection – the one with the angel. And he'll get it for very little. That's his role in the business.'

'And Marian sold . . .'

'On the cheap; I mean, who on earth would have wanted to buy stolen goods?'

'Naturally.'

'But the group needs a fallguy because, even if the story never comes out that the Palermo Caravaggio and the four segments are one and the same work, someone still has to have "discovered" the paintings. That they were found in Czechoslovakia squares perfectly. After all, it's a country which doesn't respect international treaties; anything goes in Prague. They even found that cache of Stuart pictures there recently. Seriously. Don't you remember? Those weren't stolen.'

'Yes, of course; there was also a Tintoretto and some Titians: serious stuff.'

'They need someone who, carried away by her enthusiasm – and by her dishonesty – would have openly exported masterpieces which she'd recognized out of Czechoslovakia. That this person should occupy an important position and should enjoy respect simply adds weight to the attribution, and therefore to their value in the eyes of the world. Madame Braganza "finds" them, and exports them herself. Then they disappear. It's obvious she's still got them. But they're actually in Italy, though I don't know where.'

'In Italy? How's that?'

'Because Monsignor Ermenegildo Venini and Marian Svoboda do business together: they're both legates. The Baron handed the pictures over to the Monsignor. There was the canvas which he took away with him – the one which was in Monsieur's suitcase – and then the three views of Prague were none other than the remaining Caravaggios covered over by landscapes painted in tempera so that they dried at once, and the stuff can just be removed with soap and water. Under the Moldava and the castle, there's Caravaggio's painting, the brushstrokes of Michelangelo Merisi.'

'Yes. I remember. And their dimensions looked peculiar. Yes, of course; they were the missing sections. And of course, since the San Lorenzo masterpiece was stolen well over thirty years ago, it's now legally sellable anyway.'

'The missing sections are all in Rome, but soon they'll come to England inside a diplomatic bag. Your husband will unveil them at a press conference which has already been announced – the invitations have already been sent out. Your husband wants to make a hefty profit but above all he also wants to be respected in the City. If you'll allow me to say so, respect is something he's never yet earned. If he's ever enjoyed it, it's only been reflected glory, because he's your husband. He wants to get his own back for that, and also for the abduction of his cousin, so that the ex-director of the Louvre (well, it's obvious isn't it? you'll have to resign when all the paintings appear on the market) won't be believed. The Caravaggio was found in her companion's suitcase. Yes, that was oversight on Dauphine's part. The Baron holds on to one of the sections because that's his way of keeping up with the sixth Countess Polignac-Hérisson. Two of the Caravaggios will be kept by the consortium, Caravaggio Masterpieces Ltd, and the last one'll be sold off at auction to gauge its value. Agents of the consortium have been commissioned to push up the bidding.'

'And what's Dauphine got to do with all this?'

'Your husband brought her in because he needed someone who knew your every move, who had access to your mail and telephone, who could follow you without arousing suspicion. First he tried to enlist me . . .'

Polissena looked at Valentina with open gratitude; she studied the profile of those fleshy lips, that thick hair. She wore a close-fitting black jacket fastened by a belt of fabric dyed bright blue, just like her gloves.

Lost in thought, she was looking at Valentina's face when the door opened once more and a small boy came in.

Surprised at finding the room occupied and by two women at that, he scampered away fearfully.

'There's not that much privacy . . .' ventured Valentina. But Polissena still had not finished sorting out her thoughts when the door was again pushed open. Perhaps it was her son. But no, it was Master George who, beset by nervous tics, looked at her through his thick lenses.

'At this time, parents, wives and friends should not be found in any boy's room; it's a question of their own privacy. And besides, I've already asked you, Polissena, to avoid visiting him . . .' Another muscular spasm caused his ankle to flick out in a movement such as those typically favoured by odalisques. 'The boys mustn't get distracted from their work . . .' he protested.

'You shouldn't leave your son in the hands of a neurotic and a dipsomaniac,' whispered Valentina. 'This privacy . . . well, it's a monkey-house in here! We haven't had a moment's peace since we came in. But I'll tell you this much: you've got to get rid of those Caravaggios.'

'How?'

'You've got to find out where they are soon. Now I must go; I wouldn't be surprised if they had me followed here, though I did all I could to keep them off my scent . . .'

'I don't know how to thank you, Valentina.'

'Be careful.'

Another little boy burst in. 'I wanted to borrow a book.'

He ran away at once.

'Oh! There's no peace in this room,' sighed Polissena.

174

'It's always like this,' commented a little black boy who had just come in.

But rather than a little black boy, it was in fact Boy caked in mud after playing the wall-game. 'Mama!' He had learnt to stop himself from hugging her some time ago. Not knowing what to do, they shook each other by the hand awkwardly. 'What a lovely surprise! What brings you here? No one told me. Don't let Twitch see you: he hates mothers. How's Papa? He's not been in touch for months. What are we doing these holidays?'

She looked at him gratefully. She recognized her own black eyes in the handsome and blemishless face of her child.

'You're covered in mud!'

'Mmm. There's no arguing with these ridiculous Etonian games . . .' He stepped towards the door on tiptoe. 'I'm just checking that Dame Sherry or Master Twitch aren't listening in; it's like having the KGB around here.'

'Do you really hate being here?'

'Why should I like it?'

Poor Boy. Being adolescent was a nuisance. Polissena embraced him but, on finding her blouse smudged with mud, she pushed him away at once and said, 'You're right not to eat their slops.' And she stuffed some money into his pocket in order to assuage her uneasy conscience.

The *Sunday Times* was going to publish the story in two parts: 'Unknown masterpieces returned to the West by Louvre chief'.

Baron von Wurzburg gave an interview to the *Daily Mail* all about how he had chanced upon Polissena and a friend of hers at the Czech border with a Caravaggio in their baggage. 'The gifted director of the Louvre, Madame Braganza Lockhart, wanted to safeguard the greatest discovery of the century for the sake of the European cultural heritage. In a certain sense,' it went on, 'she sacrificed herself by committing an action which was not quite honest, though it was ultimately praiseworthy.'

However, the Bohemian press and even *Pravda* accused the Louvre of stealing the canvas which rightfully belonged to the proletarian patrimony; nobody knew where the masterpieces were located – there were all of four of them! But it was felt that they must be in Madame Braganza's possession.

The Times announced an exhibition devoted to the four canvases in the hope of being asked to sponsor it. But it was Oliver who, after years of obscurity, had finally found fame on the pages of the newspapers. He had always yearned for fame, though he had never had any claim to it. Not only had he obtained notoriety, but he had also done it at Polissena's expense. 'Lockhart is the mastermind of Caravaggio Masterpieces Ltd,' announced the *Daily Express*. 'Country gentleman becomes director of artistic consortium,' detailed the *Financial Times*. 'Shares are rocketing; who wouldn't want a little piece of the Caravaggio action?' suggested the *People*.

Polissena decided to act fast, otherwise the publicity would wreck her. She did not want to be traced by the papers or the Louvre or the Minister. She had had a long talk with Dauphine. Placed under pressure, her secretary had spilled the beans. Polissena had convinced her that it was not to her disadvantage to prolong her association with that nest of vipers who were bound to end up by betraying her, and also that she was going to reward her with a promotion which would soon bring her a directorship of her own. She had asked her where the four Caravaggios were to be found.

Although she had no idea what Polissena was intending to do with those four canvases, Dauphine replied that she would tell her what she knew in exchange for one thing: Polissena would have to swear that she would fulfil her pledge without further discussion. Polissena assured her that she would give her whatever she wanted.

The four Caravaggio canvases were in the Argentinian Legation at the Holy See; Monsignor Ermenegildo Venini was legate to the Vatican. She also confirmed that the four canvases had been masked by views of Prague painted in tempera: Polissena would easily recognize them for their poor execution and their incongruous presence in such a lavish Renaissance setting. The fourth canvas, the one featuring the Madonna which Polissena had herself transported inside her car, had only just been painted over by some appalling artist who had copied the Prague town hall from a postcard.

In the Legation, which was to all intents and purposes foreign territory, the Caravaggios were on safe ground, and were only waiting to enter England via official channels;

they would announce that they had been taken directly into the English countryside – presumably to Oliver and Polissena's country house – and there they had remained during all that time.

In exchange for the information which she had divulged, Dauphine demanded that Polissena should give up R. to her.

Polissena looked at her. She was lost for words. She observed Dauphine's perfectly manicured hands, her scarf printed with horses, saddles and coats of arms. She was not expecting such a request but naturally she gave her assent to it.

VIII

In the afternoon she had told her lover that all three of them would go to a restaurant together that very evening – that is, he, herself and Dauphine de Brantes into whose hands, she confessed point blank, she had surrendered him. R. scrutinized her; he was speechless, as if he had not properly understood; he did not want to accept what his lover had just told him. 'You can only give up what's already yours,' she soothed as she stroked his mouth.

Not wishing to lose Polissena, R. had consented at once, beseeching her however to reassure him of her love. He did not want to displease her; he would always love her.

They dined in a small restaurant in Fulham, off the

beaten track. They sat down at the circular bar and ordered two martinis for the ladies and an orange juice for him. Polissena and Dauphine whispered to one another. R. barely listened to them; he had no desire to take part in the conversation and, in any case, he was not clear about what they were discussing. They went downstairs where there were only seven tables and withdrew to a corner and ordered seafood. R. ate little, unable to work up an appetite. He could see that Polissena was worried: her brow was furrowed, her black curls hung over her rather blank eyes. He sensed that Dauphine was eyeing him up lustfully, between all those lashes and lids of hers tinged in too much green. In the course of the meal, he saw Polissena pass Dauphine the key which had been attached to her necklace.

'I'll take him to Tatiana's,' she announced, as if R. was not even there. Polissena made no comment.

There was that name cropping up again.

They drank a bottle of Alsatian wine between the three of them and ate some langoustines.

On the following day R. stayed in a hotel room which Dauphine had booked for him.

He ascertained with horror that, though he loved Polissena, he could penetrate Dauphine just as she wanted and whenever she wanted with voluptuous frequency and a sorrowful longing. 'I know you love Polissena but even though you love her, you yield to both of us. You're just a thing: an item from the supermarket.' R. felt gratified to be insulted through Polissena. Dauphine offered him her big bosom and her brash voice. She offered him her most

179

intimate cavity to be kissed and sucked; in fact, she imposed it upon him and he obeyed, his groin swelling with pleasure, incapable of repressing his own acquiescence.

IX

Though neither of them was aware of the fact, they both set off for Italy at the same time: Polissena headed towards Rome and Dauphine went off with R. in tow to Venice. Polissena had to get inside the Argentinian Legation in some way without arousing suspicion: she would have to go there during a reception so that she would not set off the burglar alarm, and the state rooms would be fully illuminated. But how was she going to get to Monsignor Venini?

Luckily it was Nicholas Newman, who happened to be travelling on the very same flight, who informed her that that same evening the Legate was holding a cocktail party in honour of Pope John-Paul and, even if she had not been invited, she should come along. 'It'll be sheer theatre, real entertainment: all those terrible priests putting on their sly airs. They're all the same, eh? no? The palace itself is magnificent early Renaissance: it used to be the summer residence of Agostino Chigi – full of Roman sarcophagi, Renaissance fountains and coffered ceilings.'

'But how d'you manage to know everything, Newman?' She admired her colleague's extraordinary memory.

'In actual fact I've never been there, but I've seen pictures of it and I always remember everything I see, eh? I've refined my visual memory.' As usual, he was wearing bizarrely cut clothes; his jacket hung all over the place. 'Actually I'm going on purpose to see the Palace, the two Bellinis – Gentile, not Giovanni – the Pellegrino Tibaldi ceiling, the three drawings and the great portrait by Sebastiano del Piombo, as well as the Lotto portraits. The Monsignor has absolutely no taste: he's always got heaps of gladioli on all the tables, eh, eh? and on the writing desks he keeps photographs of Pinochet and Galtieri. But I gather he's got others tucked away in his drawers just waiting for the winds of change to blow – everything always does come back into fashion in the end. I mean, if fashion so dictated, even Beelzebub would come in, so to speak, don't you agree? And there'll be Monsignor Marcinkus at the Legation too, even if, strictly speaking, he's supposed to be arrested if he sets foot on Italian soil . . .'

'But it's Argentinian territory . . .'

'Marcinkus still has to travel through a slice of Italy to get there as the Argentinian Legation's near S. Gregorio, eh? But the ways of the Lord are infinite! No? D'you remember the de la Tour in the Reading house? I'd really love to have it . . .'

'You can have anything you want, Nicholas, as long as you take me to the Legation. I'll even leave you the de la Tour which ought really to go to the Louvre, seeing as he's a French painter. But I doubt it's still at Monpleasance; they've sold everything.'

'No décolletage: the Pope's coming.'

'Never fear.'

'He's got no fears either, eh?' He wore a smile on his greenish face. He was agreeable – not to everyone, but to her he was a friend.

'Mind you don't tell him I'm coming.'

'I wouldn't dream of it; in any case, I'm officially invited with a lady guest and, as I've no lady of my own, there won't be any trouble getting in, eh? I fear there'll also be that horrible Baron von Wurzburg there with his new Czech catamite.'

'Really?' Polissena thought that her presence might be linked to the Caravaggios. That is, as long as they had not already been despatched in some diplomatic bag. Could it be that she was too late?

'I shouldn't be telling you these things, but the Baron's just come back from Bulgaria where he had plastic surgery done to his . . . yes, well, eh, you know what I'm talking about! A small internal pump so that with a bit of manipulation, he can get it up. Apparently it's a painful operation, but many people have it done. I mean, what is one to do? When a man's reached the age of seventy, he knows everything there is to know about sex, but he can't do anything about it any more. For women it's different, eh?'

'But once the pump's been inserted, what can a man do? Can he still have orgasms?' Polissena was highly intrigued.

'No, I don't believe so, but at least he can still stuff it up some place. Forgive my crudeness, Polissena, but after all, that's what happens, isn't it? Personally I wouldn't much like to have the thing done, nor have it come into closer contact with me. But you never know!'

'Does anything come out of the pump?'

'If they could only hear us! The Directors of the Louvre and the National Gallery discussing pumps of this nature!' He burst out laughing. 'I'll come and pick you up, eh?'

In the rush she had not even booked a hotel. 'No, I'll come and pick you up, Nicholas.'

X

Dauphine had alighted at the Pontile delle Zitelle with R. following a step behind her. The Pontile was thus named because of the pious institute for poverty-stricken maidens: the convent and the church of Santa Maria della Present-azione. Alfred de Musset had been in the habit of going there to eye up the damsels embroidering their lace, and also to wander along the calli and the bridges of the Giu-decca. Amidst the greenery of the gardens, you could make out the church of Santa Croce which faced the Hyden Garden, now all blossoming and green (formerly the prop-erty of Princess Asparia of Greece); they stopped before a wall enclosing a residential building which bore the words in polished brass 'Pensione Serena'.

'We're here,' Dauphine murmured to R.; her silk scarf billowed in the wind and her greasy face-paint was smudged by the Venetian scirocco. She rang the doorbell with her gloved hand and tried to dissuade a mosquito from settling down on her bare knees. R. timorously kept back a bit from her.

The name of Tatiana Bratilova had already been invoked as a threat. Marian Svoboda had mentioned her in Prague when R. had refused his favours and Polissena had allowed him that refusal. He knew that she had lived in England and now he had found her shut into the secrecy of her boarding-house; soon he would meet her. Dauphine had never described Tatiana Bratilova or the Pensione Serena to him; but Dauphine did not talk to him much, nor did she try to explain things; maybe beneath the veneer of her silks and dressed-up designer furs and her slightly raucous voice, she was weak and timid. But R. hardly dared to think of Dauphine, or to make any judgement about her character or physical appearance, her Swiss skin or her sadistic flare-ups. He knew none of her friends; naturally he did not know who comprised her circle. She was subordinate to Polissena, and it was unlikely that they consorted with the same set of people. Polissena and Dauphine were now the only people who had a right to his body, who knew his secret. Soon Bratilova would too.

The small door opened automatically and R. followed Dauphine through a very dark corridor into a small hallway which was nearly oval in form, that is, it was as though the room were formed by two circles closed off at one end, whilst on the right-hand side, another long corridor extended in its turn; it was lined with pink silk and led to another and smaller round salon. This room went nowhere and was padded; above, the walls curved into a ceiling made of painted glass, which was mounted in overworked shapes in washed-out pinks, pale crimson and creamy magenta and which allowed very little light to filter through.

It was a suffocating atmosphere, especially during that hot September. They waited for a few minutes without Dauphine saying anything to him. She had seated herself on a bench which lined the long corridor on both sides, but R. remained standing in the small end salon with his long lashes lowered. As Donna Tatiana Bratilova entered, R. lifted his lids to look at her, to understand what it would mean to be left in the hands of that woman for some time. That much he had understood: Dauphine was going to leave him at the Pensione Serena.

Donna Tatiana gave him a passing glance but did not greet him or extend her knotty hand. Instead she welcomed Dauphine warmly. Her eyes were light brown, spoiled by the skin surrounding them: it was a very pale skin. She must have been over fifty.

'My dear Dauphine!' They shook each other by the hand. Maybe the two had been lovers thought R. as he observed them together.

Donna Tatiana offered them both a Turkish coffee in tiny cups which were brought to them by a maid with wrinkled hands and a weary back. R. felt comforted by the warm and sugary liquid which smelt of cinnamon.

Bratilova did not partake of the coffee. She got up and, turning towards Dauphine as she took R.'s hand, she asked, 'May I?'

'Please do,' answered Dauphine.

185

'Let me have a look at you, dear. It would be better if you undressed.'

'Here?' asked R.

'Remove your clothes.'

Whilst R. obeyed, embarrassed to find himself in such a place, in the presence of two dressed women and – more awkward still – in the presence of the maid who came in to collect the tray and the dirty cups swathed in her white apron over her grey alpaca skirt. But the maid – who appeared to be dumb – did not even look at him.

'Wait a moment!' Donna Tatiana rang a bell and Lakhdar appeared. He was an immensely tall man with skin the colour of light chocolate and very long, fine hands. He took the key from Dauphine's hands, unlocked the catch and freed R. from his chastity belt. 'We'll throw this one away,' Tatiana told him.

Bratilova poured herself a glass of champagne. 'Show him to us,' she told Dauphine.

She put her hands into the hollow of his groin and tried to stimulate him: she obtained an immediate reaction from him, then she made him turn around and kneel against the bench so that Donna Tatiana could get a good view of R.'s buttocks, and she opened them, revealing their most intimate secret.

The two women returned to talking between themselves whilst R. remained kneeling. Just as objects get fondled, Tatiana's knotty hand rested in inquisitorial fashion on his back and then fingered his lower belly, patting his testicles, pulling his hairs. 'Nice skin,' she commented. 'Let me see your tongue and teeth. How old are you?' She was scrutinizing him through her great gold-rimmed lenses.

'I think he's twenty-six,' Dauphine answered for him. Jerkily, twisting her thin lips as she did so, Tatiana invited Dauphine and R. to follow her into the garden; they went out via the silken corridor, passing through the small oval room which, on closer inspection, turned out to be made of two oblongs, and then they forked in the opposite direction from the one in which they had first entered, and went out into a small garden in which clumps of daisies were blooming: several pavilions could be made out between the vines and the cypress trees. Two maids wearing wide skirts and long sleeves sticky with sweat, were busying themselves between the plants carrying trays. R. gazed at their grey and anonymous faces.

'R., you do too much looking. Has no one taught you that you shouldn't observe? It's not right: it doesn't become your condition.' R. lowered his long lashes, immersing Bratilova in his blue gaze as he did so. 'You mustn't even look at me, or at Madame. You need some modesty; you can stare at your colleagues, but not at us!' It was explained to him that he could look at the women from the waist down, but he was not supposed to look into their faces; were he to be caught in the act of scrutinizing his owner, he would be punished.

They passed through a coloured archway into a courtyard around which were distributed several rooms, like in a convent or a madrasa.

'Yours, R., bears the initials of Madame DdB. Breakfast and lunch are consumed in the cells. There are four other lodgers in the villa at the moment: you'll meet them later. We all eat together in the evenings, but we never go out unless you insist on having a walk around Venice but, in that case, you'll have to be escorted by Amos or Lakhdar. If you need to know anything, you're to ask Amos, and if you need anything in particular, you can address your request to either one of them.' R. remembered to keep his eyes glued to her waist. 'There's no telephone at Villa Serena.'

Dauphine listened, observing Bratilova with folded arms. Donna Tatiana had exhausted peroxide hair. The longest locks fell on her neck, which was rounded by a spartan collar, but two diamonds sparkled on her earlobes.

'You do know you've been yielded and that you must do whatever Madame asks of you, don't you?' R. nodded: he would obey. 'Kneel.' He was naked and felt still more undressed under the indifferent gaze of Donna Tatiana. 'Do you consent to wear the monogram with which Dauphine de Brantes desires you to be marked?'

Subjecting himself brought him pleasure even though he knew that the more ground he surrendered, the more demanding their requests would become. 'I consent.'

Dauphine took him by the shoulders. Her painted face shone ecstatically; she squeezed his groin. She kissed him as if caught in a sudden hurry and she left, almost running, her silk shoes kicking up behind her. R. was grateful for that embrace. Maybe she loved him, maybe – knowing him to be hers — she was beginning to feel affection for him, passion even. He raised his eyes. In the middle of the courtyard rose a tower with a rounded base; it rose up far higher than the cells and culminated in a sort of mushroom-shaped room. It was the tower where the boarders were whipped, one of his companions told him later. But there was also the music room which opened on one side of the courtyard and which had a singular type of entrance. 'Nicky de St Phalle designed that; she's one of my dearest friends,' Bratilova had explained, but R. did not react; he had never heard of that strange name, and the result of her labours struck him as bizarre. Come to that, all the architecture of the boarding-house struck him as irrational and unusual, but he did not ask questions any more; by now, he just looked and accepted. Not that R. had ever asked many questions in the past: R. had never been inquisitive, nor had he ever been an observer: he was accustomed not to comment. Things and people had passed him by without leaving any trace in his memory; he could not even remember the furniture which adorned Monpleasance, or the colour of Polissena's eyes or the paintings which Nicholas Newman had talked about.

In the morning, just as Madame Bratilova had outlined, R. ate breakfast in his room which was pleasingly decorated with a couple of pieces of painted Venetian furniture and a modern chair. Both the meals were brought in by one of the maids, Rina or Nanda, tired and dusty spinsters both of them. The trays were well disposed with dishes of silver and porcelain which contained concentrated clam juices, protein pills, powdered vitamins and extract of lettuce. It was rather boring fare, as indeed were many of the hours passed at Villa Serena. He had requested to go out for a walk: he could hardly recall anything about Venice, which was why he would have liked to visit St Mark's Square and see the pigeons. But Lakhdar had started preparing him: he had attached a gold chain around his neck. Walking amidst the tourists in such a guise, with that Watussi figure leading him on a chain, struck him as undignified and he gave up the idea of a promenade.

It has already been described how, from the pavilion which opened on to the tower, through an entrance jutting out towards the strange campanile, you entered into the gymnasium, a rounded pavilion where the boarders exercised their bodies. They did this in order to firm up their flexor, extensor, rotatory, abductor, adductor and sphincter muscles, and also to increase and strengthen their pectorals, their triceps, their stomach support muscles and, in particular, to exercise their so-called sexual muscles, and not just the gluteus maximus.

The boarding-house was equipped with various medical electronic machines which sucked and pulled the youths' phalli, and then stretched them by means of a piston action, an exercise which the lodgers were obliged to perform for twenty minutes every morning and an hour in the afternoon in order to lengthen and reinforce and increase the size of their organs. The results were so prodigious that they alarmed even their own subjects since Riccardo, Gianni, R., Hubert and Angelo knew that they would have to administer these huge pieces of meat growing between their legs upon one another; such was their newly acquired size that they had to force their entrance into the sphincter, a process which was excruciatingly painful. Their sphincters were also exercised and made to contract and relax by Amos who gave instructions following a record which dictated the one-two-three beat so that the gluteal gymnastics were always accompanied by rhythmic music. Little by little the lodgers succeeded in enclosing every kind of object to the point where Amos, for instance, could no longer withdraw his arm, so tight was the contraction of that orifice. Riccardo had even managed to keep two arms inside him.

Inside the tower, however, the boarders would be kept chained with their arms and legs extended and fitted into leather straps fastened to the various marble columns built into the middle of the room for this very purpose.

Not all of the four youths with whom R. shared his sojourn at the Villa Serena were new to such exercises; some of them came back to Bratilova every year for a week at a time, and there were some lady-owners who left them with Donna Tatiana whenever they travelled abroad, as is customary with domestic pets. They were slaves to these women, trained to every kind of abuse.

The high walls which surrounded the garden of Villa Serena and separated it from the calli and the bridges, enclosing the music which issued from the gymnasium at top volume, guaranteed the isolation of the boarding house. Now and then some hapless tourist would come along with his family; having failed to find lodging in the other boarding houses of the Giudecca, he might turn to this one in the hope of a bed and some breakfast for himself and his children. They might see the maids with their grey hair fastened in a white cap, their long aprons reaching down to their ankles, and they would regret not finding any room in such a pleasantly quaint spot. But if, instead, the tourist was confronted by Amos or Lakhdar, he would make double sure to find lodging elsewhere, even if it meant staying in Mestre: anything so long as he did not have to linger a moment longer in the little boarding house.

Amos, the older Watussi, was always shrouded in the shadows of doors, cupboards, cypress trees: he seemed omnipresent. R. would catch those black eyes like the eyes of a goat staring at him.

'Bring him to me,' Tatiana ordered him, indicating R. with her long chin. Bratilova's face had something equine about it, especially with that damaged yellow hair. At her gesture, two of the boarders rushed to his side. Bratilova observed the marks on his body. 'Who whipped you? Was it Madame or Dauphine?' When she was absent, she referred to his new mistress by her first name. 'Madame' or 'Madama' was reserved for Polissena.

'Dauphine.'

'What did she use?'

'The lash,' he replied without looking at her.

'You'll be whipped this afternoon in the tower, then we'll leave you alone till they mark you. Riccardo,' she addressed the naked youth on R.'s right. He was hirsute, covered in black hair, but even through his thick curls, you could still make out the stripes, the wounds administered by the whip. Part of Riccardo's chest had been shaved in the shape of a letter of the alphabet: 'His lover's initial,' Amos – who did not otherwise utter a word – had explained. They had also shaved his pubic area entirely, using the wax method. 'It's much more painful than the whip,' Riccardo had confessed to him, 'but my mistress wants me this way. She says I look more naked, more hers.' Gianni instead was covered in tattoos, some of which were 'home-made'; once he had even asked for two pudding moulds with metal edges which the maids kept in the kitchen, and he had heated up the metal rims and then he had them applied to his pectorals; the moulds had left two terrible star-shaped scars of which Gianni was very proud. He carried his own nakedness boldly and it was he who planned the order of the day. Before meeting his owner he had worked in a travel agency specializing in groups, conventions and low-budget holidays. He would, with dedication and a certain measure of mastery, try to vary the programme, even if during those days at Villa Serena, there was little to vary.

PENSIONE SERENA:
Tuesday

Morning: breakfast in cell
newspapers
shower
rest

| | music-room: gymnastics and various exercises |
| | massage |

Afternoon:	lunch in cell
	rest
	meeting in garden
	conversation
	bath or jacuzzi

Evening:	dinner in garden or dining room (subject to
	weather and mosquitoes)
	thrashing in the tower – various tortures and
	concert
	coffee or tisane

Sometimes the black and sinister Lakhdar, his eyes yellow in the gloom of the garden, would play the flute like something out of Henri Rousseau.

'Let's draw lots,' proposed Bratilova who did not always dine with the boarders, or else was present at both the exercises and the floggings. 'Let's see which of you will be tied up. Leave R. out of it as he can't be touched for a few days and deal out the cards to all.'

Angelo, a little blond boy whose body was literally covered in lashmarks so that he looked just like a grilled steak, had a handsome, virile face. 'But the loveliest of all of you is R.,' Donna Tatiana kept on repeating as she looked at him through her big lenses. 'But Hubert is lovely too!' Hubert was a half-caste who looked rather gloomy but who did in fact have a very cheerful disposition. It was indeed

194

Hubert who was selected as victim and R. was chosen to execute the ritual gestures. He tied his arms behind his back with a silken cord and, pushing him ahead, he took him up to the tower.

Hubert bore the symbol of his slavery on his body. 'My lover wanted me to have the operation.' But Hubert was very proud of it. When completely naked, his body revealed a belt tied to his waist and supported by two small openings cut into his flesh. 'You too must submit yourself to an operation. Yours will be agonizing: we know you've already consented.'

R. had to accept that it was his duty, but also his pleasure and his very raison d'être to do so. The terrible day approached: it would come soon; he trembled at the mere thought of it but, at the same time, the idea of it thrilled him with painful delight. He thought of it at night and during mealtimes. He had by now forgotten what good food tasted like: all those dinners flowing with wine of which he had partaken with Polissena, but now – he was ashamed to admit it – it was Dauphine whom he considered his owner; Polissena's image came vaguely back to mind now and then, causing him something akin to embarrassment because he had forgotten and replaced her so easily.

Where on earth was Polissena now?

Between the myrtle and laurel bushes and the acanthus leaves expertly illuminated by concealed light sources, the guards in formal dress protecting the Argentinian Legation scrutinized the brocade-ridden, medal-wearing guests who came crowned by back-combed, dyed and false hair. A flailing plume on their cocked hats, the men at arms recognized the members of the Curia, the government, the press and the *sottogoverno*. But they had received peremptory notice to recognize Marcinkus on any account, given that they would then have had to arrest him. They looked at Polissena on Newman's arm; he appeared green and nervous. Polissena had sewn a stiff rose on to her silk mantle and her legs emerged from the curling hem which was cut at the knee to a dressmaker's length as haute couture dictated. Together they ascended the travertine marble steps with busts of Roman emperors and Renaissance nobles at every landing. 'You don't look a bit like the others,' commented Newman as he brushed past the candyfloss ladies and the toy ladies and the lady MPs built like tanks, or the wives of Christian Democrat MPs with white and damaged hair, and Lebanese women swathed in veils, the wives of new industrialists. With his awkwardly dangling jacket, Newman did not look like anyone in there either; his jacket was grubby, with the hems unstitched and capped by that green face.

Smart and shiny, her lips thickened by the usual dark

lipstick, her eyes worried, her high forehead hidden under her wavy hair, her hands around a glass, Polissena slipped away from Newman's arm. Before she distanced herself from Nicholas and thus interrupted his recitation of exclamations and isn't that trues?, he had advised her not to miss the Annibale Carracci which covered the ceiling of the fourth room on the right and to look out for the Pellegrino Tibaldi, nor to forget to seek out the Sebastiano del Piombo. Two statues indicated the true entrance but Polissena could not make out Monsignor Venini whom she did not know in any case and would not therefore have recognized. But she wanted to avoid being noticed and the Monsignor was not performing the honours of the house because he had apparently retired into the room of the angels (so called because it was frescoed with images of sprightly angels) in the company of Wojtyla to talk about East European politics and about how to raise the funds with which to pay for the Pope's never-ending round of foreign travels; the Pope was fast emptying the coffers of St Peter's obuli. The Monsignor was trying to convince His Holiness to sell some of the Vatican pictures – there were so many in reserve – nobody would notice if the canvases left via the Legation.

She would go hunting for the Caravaggios at once, decided Polissena; she had no time to lose. Besides, as the director of a museum and also in her capacity as an art historian, she had every excuse to examine the pictures, scan the walls and the frescoes. She passed three swarms of prelates, crowds of cardinals, masses of women dressed in dismal black, P2 members who had gone out of fashion, had now become a little deaf and were to be seen bowed over the hands of Eminences, kissing their profusion of rings. 'There are sixty-three cardinals but not a drop of champagne!' complained the first secretary of the Farnese Palace.

Polissena let her disorientated eye travel between one Rosso Fiorentino tapestry and another Lorenzo Lotto portrait, admiring the coffered ceilings, lowering her gaze to the signed photographs which were frequently dedicated to Monsignor Venini by former royalty, prime ministers and dictators. Above the signed image of Evita Peron there hung an amorous scene by Pellegrino Tibaldi and a portrait of Vittoria Colonna executed by Sebastiano del Piombo. So that was where it was! thought Polissena who had vainly sought that portrait, the location of which had remained unknown. Tuberoses and gladioli and silver ashtrays lined the rooms crowded with petitioners in purpurin robes, with old foot-draggers: it was like being in the ante-room of Francesco Sforza or Federico Gonzaga during the darkest years of the Renaissance. You had to grapple your way between Bianca Maria Fanfani and Giulio Andreotti who were not talking to each other, and between the waiters who were readily confused with the American cardinals being less theatrically dressed than their Italian counterparts; she threaded her way between the dwarfish members of Parliament in order to pass from one drawing room to another, always on the look-out for the views of Prague. Her heart was in turmoil, her breath came short, her sweaty hands squeezed the glass she held and her knees gently trembled. She vividly remembered those three that she had seen at the Bohemian border in the Baron's possession. The fourth, the 'new' one, had been painted over the Madonna, and depicted Prague town hall. The four canvases hung over the flowery upholstered sofas.

How was Polissena going to get rid of those people sitting under them?

'The Prime Minister's just come in,' she announced turning towards everyone and no one in particular, her voice loaded with fictitious enthusiasm.

'Which one?'

'The Italian Prime Minister . . .'

'He's only in charge for another couple of days: it's not worth the trouble . . .' came the reply.

'He's done for – they're getting rid of him tonight.'

They had no intention of moving.

'Oh! But he's with the Pope,' she ventured.

They all got up. The Pope still generated some interest, even if he was to be seen every day all over the world, on every television screen.

'Where?'

'Down there: in the entrance . . .'

'I kissed his hand last year,' said one old man.

'Come on: let's go and see him . . .'

'Come on, come on,' responded the old lawyer wearily raising himself from the sofa and almost hitting his head against the Moldava. Within a few seconds they had all gone.

Polissena locked the door and, dispensing with her glass — which contained only mineral water anyway — she removed the first picture from the wall and deposited it on the balcony. It was the long one, about 150 cm by 40 cm: under the mediocre tempera there was one beautiful saint with his head bowed towards the Christ child, and the draperies — beautiful and flowing — already prefiguring Zurbarán.

She removed the second painting which hung between the sofa and a table. It measured 45 cm by 45 cm. It was certainly the mutilated angel with the advertising placard proclaiming Gloria in Excelsis Deo which the Baron so craved for his own collection. Polissena remembered it well, that Neapolitan street-urchin angel with his right hand tensed towards the sky, his young face turned towards the Madonna and Child; the other arm pointed towards the head of the Madonna almost to the extent of touching her, so underlining where the centre of action was to be found, thus achieving the perfect composition. Polissena took the canvas in her hands and carried it to the balcony, leaning it against the other one. From her handbag she extracted a small bottle and, with her lighter at the ready, she sprayed the canvases with paraffin. Then she ignited them.

The fire caught straight away on the old dry canvas and, as the stratum of tempera disappeared beneath the flames and was eaten up by them, the magical brushworks were revealed to her eyes, together with the colours and shapes between the pools of light licked by the flames, which then vanished again in a flash.

There was no time for enchantment before those master-pieces: the guests might come back into the drawing room at any moment and find the door locked, or the guards might see the flames on the balcony from below.

It was time for the third canvas: St Lawrence and St Francis, those who had once been at the Madonna's right hand adoring the Child. The canvas measured some 35 cm by 50 cm. Then, finally, Polissena unhooked the picture she knew so well, the only one which she had seen in its original state that day at the frontier: it was a perfectly square-shaped canvas. Under Prague town hall languished the Madonna lit from below by a blue and sinister light; her left hand was leaning on the manger, whilst the other was modestly folded: it was the face of a young Sicilian girl.

She carried it to the balcony and sprayed it with paraffin: the nourished flame blazed around its two new victims and crackled amidst the black smoke; the other two canvases were by now almost totally consumed.

For a moment Polissena saw the face of the Madonna emerge between the flames. She did not linger and, in a release of emotion, and also perhaps out of sadness, she wept.

In a few seconds there was nothing left but a few ashes and some smoke. She shut the balcony windows so that the bonfire should not be discovered immediately, and turned the key in the lock; she walked once again from one draw-ing room to another, but this time it was in the opposite direction from the one in which she had first come. As she passed in front of the portrait of Vittoria Colonna, she saw

Marian Svoboda who was seated between prelates.

The lawyer who had got up from the sofa and had almost hit his head against the painting of the Moldava, stopped her with one hand. 'We didn't find him!'

'Who?' she asked in terror. She did not want Marian to see her: she wanted to leave as quickly as possible.

'The Pope.'

'Really? But he was on Monsignor Venini's arm.'

'No, that's impossible: Ermenegildo Venini's over there, sitting down: can't you see him? He was there before as well.'

Polissena turned in the direction indicated by the lawyer and saw Marian Svoboda. 'Is that Venini?' she asked in astonishment.

'Of course!'

'You're quite sure you're not mistaken?'

'How could I be wrong? The Monsignor is my client as well as our host this evening. But excuse my asking, who was it invited you to the Legation?'

Polissena stared at Marian dressed up as a Monsignor. Now she understood the game at last.

The embarrassing exchange was interrupted by Newman. 'Where did you finish up? eh?' His green face was highly animated. 'Have you seen the Carracci, the Tibaldi, the Rosso Fiorentino?' No, she had seen the Caravaggio instead.

'I must dash – I'm in a hurry . . .'

'You can't possibly not have a look at the Pellegrino Tibaldi ceiling. Come with me: it's one of the most beautiful sights in the world, it's true, eh? He's a great painter, that one, eh? Lucky old Monsignor Venini; there he is, living in splendour, amongst such wonders . . . But Polissena, you've got red eyes. Have you been crying? Why were you crying, eh? Is that why you want to go?'

'It's the cigarette smoke – I can't stand it.' She rushed down the steps to weep from the bottom of her heart, to sob amidst the laurels and acanthus. To think that it should have been her to burn one of the greatest masterpieces of European painting, to sacrifice that magnificent and perverse work by Caravaggio for the sake of her own interests; it was infuriating. But she had been forced to do it, she told herself. At the same time, she pitied herself and went on crying as she had not done for years.

In the meantime, the firemen had been called because the gardener had seen a burst of flame on one of the balconies of the palace.

But when they arrived, they found nothing, and they left disappointed.

XII

One morning Bratilova addressed him, 'Let me have a good look at you.' She inserted her hand between his buttocks and scrutinized him carefully as she touched his most intimate crevices, opening up his backside as you would do to a beast at the market. R. did not feel hurt: he realized that he no longer belonged to himself: he knew that his body had been surrendered.

Sometimes, at night, Bratilova would send for one of the boarders and have herself caressed. When it was his turn or rather, when R. was asked to perform the task, he would steal glances at those old eyes fixed upon the ceiling, at her thin lips closed in a continuous spasm, and he would think of the terrible day awaiting him.

Bratilova did not give herself up to anybody. She consumed the hand which touched her, the warm wet tongue of the other person who might just as well have been any one of the boarders. They said that she had once had an adored female companion with whom she had passed several magical months until something tragic had happened; maybe the girl had died or maybe she had left her; since that time, Bratilova had never again succeeded in loving anyone. R. doubted that that woman with the equine features and the glacial stare could ever have actually felt real passion for a person. But Tatiana did enjoy pressing R.'s head against her belly as if to keep him prisoner. He had never seen her naked; she never removed her nightdress and, towards dawn, she would send him away.

Once, as he caressed Donna Tatiana – she remained beneath the sheets as he exposed his open legs – he had felt Amos' gaze fixed upon him from the shadows of a corner. He had motioned for him to go: he was ashamed to be seen performing the act of stroking the patronne and bringing her to satisfaction, with himself remaining passive, but Tatiana had rebuked him: he had no right to order anybody to do anything, she told him.

Once, when he was in an even more indiscreet position, the two old maids, Rina and Nanda, had surprised him — they always wore their grey alpaca skirts under their cotton aprons during those fiery September days. Bratilova had in fact made him kneel with his arms leaning on the bedside table and, whilst with one hand she kept his buttocks apart, she plunged the other into his muscular ring and pushed it into his body, provoking in him acute pain. What is more, as R. caught sight of Rina looking at him, his muscles contracted.

'Relax,' Bratilova had ordered.

But as she ascertained that R. was embarrassed in the presence of the two old maids who feigned not to see the kneeling man thus penetrated, and they went on dusting the furniture with a feather brush, Donna Tatiana pressed her arm in deeper and then withdrew it again, crucifying him with pain. On another occasion, she had commanded him to masturbate in front of Lakhdar. The function itself was far from aesthetic, nor was it remotely dignified, R. had responded. At which, Bratilova had called in all the other lodgers, Amos and Lakhdar and the two old maids and, under threat of terrible punishment, she had obtained what she wanted from him.

One morning she told him, 'Dauphine will be here today.' And she ordered him back to his cell to sleep for a couple of hours.

Dauphine arrived towards midday. She kissed him, stayed with him, touching him with her gloved hand, contemplating him as he writhed beneath the lash. She had undressed in the garden of the Pensione Serena, throwing all that precious silk to the ground so that she could enjoy him all the better, kissing him on the mouth and entreating him not to mess up her hair. 'I've just been to the hairdresser,' she told him. Dauphine's passion was always of limited duration. In the evening, she had herself taken as she was, dressed, in front of everyone, lifting her skirt which revealed her as ready for him and his companions. As R. had plunged himself into her, Riccardo had wedged himself between them and caressed Dauphine's bosom, sucking her and playing between her buttocks.

R. delighted in the cruel and thrusting impulse of Dauphine's body, in her hunger for him. But she reproached him for his superficiality. 'Aren't you ashamed? You take me as if Polissena had never existed.'

But she was wrong.

R. hoped that one day Polissena would come back to fetch him or that, through Dauphine, Polissena would realize his total obedience and would still love him. He also hoped that one day, at the sight of Dauphine with all her signed designer accessories, naked and full of lust and with her hair all dressed up, he would no longer feel any desire for her. He would let himself be thrashed, but he would not feel any longing for her, and she would be humiliated and understand. Instead his body punctually directed his blood towards his belly every time, and his desire throbbed inside its visibly swollen head.

After all that exercise, his phallus had become gigantic. Dauphine complimented Bratilova as she weighed him up between her hands. 'Much better now,' she kept repeating.

'And he'll be even bigger in a week's time,' Tatiana had assured her.

Then Dauphine had gone and the routine exercises had started up again. 'Only a few days left,' Bratilova warned him. And his companions said as much too: 'Soon it'll be your turn.'

Dauphine returned. 'Has he been told quite what must be done to him?' she asked, fingering his groin as if he were some kind of animal, without even looking at him, but turned towards Bratilova.

Bratilova's hair, which was dyed the colour of straw, and her gold-rimmed glasses sent off splinters of reflected light into the garden of Villa Serena. She had a sports-man's muscles.

'Didn't Madame say anything about it to you?' asked Bratilova, and she took R. by the hand and stroked his suntanned shoulders. 'Seeing as you belong to her, you'll be marked with her initials,' she confided; 'DdB, Dauphine de Brantes. You'll be marked. Do you accept?'

R. accepted for he had no other option and besides, he had already given his consent; Dauphine, who was in Venice for the Biennale festival, was to return for the ritual spectacle.

When, that same night, standing by Tatiana's side, R. had said, 'Though I've never been tattooed before, the prospect does not frighten me that much,' she had replied, 'But my poor lad, it's not a tattoo: you'll be branded with fire. Dauphine de Brantes sent me her irons yesterday.' They had been designed by Armani. 'Branded?' echoed R.

in terror. And he was unable to sleep a wink.

He was not whipped during those days so that his skin would heal completely, but he was ordered to administer the lash on the others. He surprised himself in performing the task with ever greater gusto especially when it came to Angelo, the little blond boy who was the gentlest, whose white skin flushed immediately with blood and whose screams induced them to plead to him to stop. The whip always left him with bloody marks on his inside thigh as Gianni and Riccardo kept his legs apart. R. would ignore Angelo's pleas; anyway, even if Bratilova was not there to keep time, there was always Amos to tell him, 'Still six more minutes,' or 'Another twenty-five.'

Gianni's floggings were also suspended as he too had to undergo an operation. His owner wanted him to wear two rings beneath her initials. The first, the heavier one, had to pierce the skin of his testicles; it supported the second which was linked to the first. The rings would be soldered together in front of the owner who was to come over specially from Rio de Janeiro where she lived. Except that, at the moment, his flesh was still getting accustomed to the new weight of the metallic body which pierced it.

Gianni was very proud of it, but R. had not been able to contemplate the moment when he would be tortured and, when the maids came to fetch him from his cell one morning, washing him thoroughly and shaving him; when they also handed him a generous glass of cognac, he understood that the moment had come. He was tottering as he entered the tower.

In the middle of the room, he saw that they had placed

a kind of altar upon which burned a small brazier and around which were positioned all his companions as well as Bratilova and Dauphine.

Dauphine indicated where she wanted R. to be branded and Bratilova asked Amos and Lakhdar to tie R. down securely at the waist with a very tight belt which attached him firmly to one of the columns: it felt cold against his stomach. He sensed the fire crackling, he could see the red-hot iron. His arms and his hands were also secured by a leather strap. Riccardo, Gianni, Angelo and Hubert sat down around him as in a show, though they were also embarrassed and fearful. He could feel the thongs pulling on his ankles, his neck: he could not move a millimetre. A load of terror blurred his vision and dried his throat; though it paralysed him, his terror also tickled his groin. Dauphine showed him the design with which he was to be branded on both his buttocks. R. was trembling and keeping his eyes lowered, but he glimpsed Bratilova plunging the red-hot iron into his flesh and keeping it there for a few seconds whilst his blood scorched. The stabbing pain transfixed him: it rent his body into a sunburst from the point where the iron fried his blood, spreading throughout his limbs, accumulating in his eyes, his brain, becoming ever greater. As his knees collapsed beneath the straps, his other buttock was marked by fire. In that moment, R. fainted from the pain.

A week went by before he recovered; he suffered and thought of distant Monpleasance, and Dauphine who did not return.

EPILOGUE

Polissena turned up to the press conference wearing black and white; she looked like a Vasarely. She was accompanied by her lawyer and two policemen in plain clothes. She had already told everything – or almost everything – to Inspector Roberts of Scotland Yard.

In front of the representatives of the press, in front of Oliver (against whom she had initiated divorce proceedings), in front of Dauphine and Baron von Wurzburg, she had taken her oath and told the story of how she had found herself caught in a trap which had been deliberately set for her. It was a dramatic scene, with Polissena at the microphone accusing, addressing and persuading those present. The paintings by Caravaggio, the existence of which had been assured by Caravaggio Masterpieces Ltd, had not appeared because they no longer existed. They had been burned in a sad incident caused by the inadvertence of a thoughtless and anonymous smoker at the Argentinian Legation to the Vatican. Yes, because it was there that the four masterpieces were kept! Oliver had protested in that faltering manner inculcated by aristocratic boarding schools that the masterpieces were not in fact sections from the

'Nativity' stolen from the Oratory of S. Lorenzo in Palermo: Madame Braganza – his wife – had gone along with the scheme from the start; it would not have been possible without her. But Dauphine had already deposited a signed statement with the police in which she had admitted everything: she had kept her side of the bargain. But Polissena did not stick to her pledge. She did not promote Dauphine de Brantes as she had promised and what is more, she sacked her in a storm of scandal and obtained from the Ministry the assurance that Mademoiselle de Brantes would never again find employment in France. Valentina was instead rewarded and promoted. The Ministry offered its apologies to Polissena and recommended her for the Légion d'Honneur, first class.

Then Polissena – the crease on her brow had finally disappeared – had gone to Venice to take possession of R. They were to go back to Monpleasance, she told him reassuringly. They were going to transform the castle into a centre, maybe a touch less exotic than the one at Hloboke, but more elegant without a doubt. In any case, Lady Isabella and the Marquis would never realise – or they would pretend not to understand – the reason for so many comings and goings of guests to the seventeenth-century apartments of the castle.

Before doing so, poor R. had to submit himself to a second trial by fire in order to transform the DdB into PB which turned out not to be too difficult. After all, how would Polissena have been able to consort with him if she had to touch the initials of her former secretary every time, seared on the buttocks of her object?

And so ends the adventurous story of R. who remained by Polissena's side, content to be the object of such an able woman who was not only director of the Louvre, but also President of the Monpleasance College, of which R. himself was Vice-President. The earnings derived from this second enterprise were going to amount to at least ten times the sum which Polissena brought home from the Louvre, and it was in this way that the two of them became rather rich.

Too much time and too many events had gone by since the first time Polissena had noticed the great blue eyes scanning her timidly, for her now to pluck up the courage and the effrontery to ask him his name.

The summer was then drawing to a close.